IMPERFECT

by Ryan Field

A Male/Male Erotic Romance

A Ryan Field Press© Original Publication
Printed by CreateSpace
Cover and Book Formatting by:
www.glendalepubservices.com

Published By: Ryan Field Press©
On the World Wide Web at:
www.ryan-field.blogspot.com

CONTENTS

CHAPTER ONE

After he paid the driver and climbed out of the taxi, Rider Evans looked up at the tall buildings and sighed. Then he slammed the back door and the taxi pulled away with a screech. Anther taxi sped by and a thin young guy with a lumberjack beard and a man bun screamed a pejorative at someone on a bicycle. Horns honked; engines roared. Someone bumped into him and didn't stop to apologize. The passersby on the sidewalk and in the street either stared at their phones or trudged forward without looking sideways. Even though it was late October and there was a chill in the air, it felt thick and oppressive and smelled of steamy bus fumes and burnt pretzel dough.

Rider turned toward the entrance of the Knickerbocker building and stepped onto the sidewalk. If he hadn't been summoned there for this important meeting he never would have left West Hollywood. He hadn't been back in New York since he'd graduated from college…two years…and he realized he missed nothing about it.

The elevator stopped on the 29th floor and he stepped out, turned right, and headed for the office at the end of a long hall that had been decorated sparsely in several different shades of taupe. The generic paintings hanging on the wall tried too hard to imitate mid-century modern abstracts and they reminded him of every other long hallway he'd ever walked down in a Manhattan high rise.

When he reached the end of the hall, he stopped and smiled at the sign on the door. It read, "Rainbow Palm Productions," in bright gold letters with a jet black background. To the right of the letters a bright gold palm tree logo swaying to the right made him smile even wider. Such a shiny, exotic name for a company located in such a glum location crossed the lines of irony and veered into absurdity.

Rider wasn't complaining, not by any means. He'd been lucky to get a job with Rainbow Palm Productions fresh out of college. Most of the people with whom he'd graduated were still waiting tables or working in retail jobs. There weren't that many opportunities out there for recently graduated new adults just starting out in the world, let alone openly gay guys who didn't feel the need to remain in the closet. Rider had student loans to pay, and the last thing he wanted to do was move back home with his family and tweet from the basement. So he opened the door, stepped into the office, and flashed his biggest, brightest smile at the receptionist.

Of course she was glancing down at her desk and talking to another young man who looked as if he was ready to leave the office. Rider stopped smiling and looked around the reception area and frowned again. It was as bland and dismal as the rest of the building, with the expected black leather sofas and chairs, flanked with chrome and glass tables.

At first glance, the large window behind the receptionist exposed an impressive view of lower Manhattan, but then Rider started to wonder how long it would take for that novelty to wear off. He figured a person could only look at gray and steel for so long before it became invisible, and he imagined the receptionist probably hadn't even glanced at that view in months.

The other young man was about the same age as Rider, with darker, longer hair he'd parted straight down the middle...a mistake.

The other guy sent Rider a seductive glance and smiled. "Well, hello," he said.

Rider nodded and smiled in his direction without saying anything.

The receptionist handed the guy a small card with something she'd written on it and said, "You can check back in about a week, but I can't promise you a definite appointment."

The guy shrugged and said, "Thank you. I'll give it a try." As he turned to leave, he looked Rider up and down again, licked his lips, and smiled all the way out the door.

Rider figured the guy was trying to get an appointment with Boris Knickerbocker, the same person Rider was seeing that morning. Boris was the great grandson of one of the wealthiest industrialists of the 20th century, and the namesake to that very high rise Rider was standing in at that moment. The Knickerbocker family was worth billions now, and they'd allowed Boris to create Rainbow Palm Productions as a way to support him for being an openly gay man. In all fairness, it wasn't just a hobby for Boris, and Rider had always respected him for that. Boris wasn't one of those spoiled trust fund guys who tinkered with this and that just for fun. He'd graduated with a law degree from one of the best Ivy League universities in the country, and he was determined to make Rainbow Palm Productions a viable, profitable business that would serve the LGBTQ community.

The receptionist glanced over at Rider and asked, "May I help you?" She was one of those attractive young women who wore black all the time, but unfortunately had her hair cut in a short, blunt trendy style that made her face appear too round and small. The dark purple-red hair color didn't help.

Rider took a breath and walked over to her desk. "I'm here to see Mr. Knickerbocker, please."

She lifted her head and smiled. "*Everyone's* here to see Mr. Knickerbocker. Do you have an appointment, honey?" Rider thought it was a shame she didn't let her hair grow a little longer.

"Just tell him Rider Evans is here," he said. Then he turned to face Boris's door. He'd never felt comfortable around people who call total strangers *honey*.

"Oh, Mr. Evans," she said. "It's so nice to meet you. I should have recognized you from your Twitter Avi. I'm so sorry. I'm a huge fan of your work. I've read everything you've ever done, and I'm a huge fan of your tweets." Then she stood up and crossed the room to Boris's door. "I'll tell him you're here."

Rider smiled and said, "Thank you." He almost laughed. It always amazed him when people thought his tweets were so fascinating. He'd never taken more than a second or two to think about anything he'd tweeted. He'd always worked hard on his assignments, but social media was something he did because it gave him more web exposure. And he thought his Twitter Avi was one of the worst photos he'd ever taken. He kept telling himself he had to get a better one soon.

A moment later, the receptionist escorted him into Boris's office and he found Boris sitting behind a huge dark walnut banker's desk. In direct contrast to the rest of the stark, modern high rise, Boris's office resembled the most exaggerated judge's chambers ever designed. There were red leather Queen Anne wing chairs and plush Asian carpets. The walls had been paneled in the same dark walnut as the desk, and heavy dark red damask draperies hung from the wall of windows. Boris had even had a gas fireplace installed, with a mantel that rivaled those usually found in gentleman's clubs.

When Boris glanced up from his desk and saw Rider standing there, he stood up and practically ran across the room to hug him. As the receptionist closed the door behind her, Boris threw his arms around Rider and said, "It's been too long. You look even handsomer now than you did the last time I saw you. I'm still not sure why you're not a male model. I'll never understand that. You'd make a fortune in modeling."

Rider refrained from rolling his eyes and hugged him. "It's good to see you, too, Boris. It feels just like old times." They'd been lovers once, or at least for a while they thought that's what they were. When they both realized they'd never been anything more than fuck buddies, they continued having sex and became best friends without a hint of any future romantic relationship. This was long before Boris had hired Rider to work for his company, back when Rider had been a freshman in college. Boris was about ten years older than Rider and he'd been teaching a course at Rider's college one semester and they'd wound up in bed after Boris's third lecture. It was the year Rider learned that spectacular sex and intimacy don't always go together as they lead people to believe in movies and TV shows.

Boris took a step back and gestured to one of the red leather wing chairs. "Have a seat, buddy. Is there anything I can get you? Would you like a drink? Something to eat? Anything you want, just name it."

Rider smiled and walked over to one of the wing chairs. He sat down, crossed his legs, and said, "I'm fine, thank you. You're looking well."

"Are you sure?" Boris asked, ignoring the compliment. He spoke with an animated voice and smiled too much. "I can have anything you want sent up. Did I tell you how great you look?"

Rider smiled again. "Yes. I believe you did tell me how great I look. You look great, too." Boris was 34 years old but didn't look a day over 25. He'd never been one of those naturally attractive model types, but he'd always worked hard to look his best. That's one of the reasons Rider had slept with him in the first place. He had a nice, slim body, but not a gym body with bulging muscles. His dark blond hair was thinning a little but his chest was as hairy as his legs. He resembled so many other young generic straight married men Rider had always found his daddy appeal hard to resist. He was also an aggressive but quiet lover.

"You look as if you've been working out a lot more," Boris said. He walked over and squeezed Rider's bicep.

Rider reached up and grabbed Boris's crotch. He squeezed his dick and said, "Just what do you want, Boris. I know you too well to play these games. Remember, I've sucked your dick."

"And you did it very well I might add."

"And don't you forget it," Rider said. "Now what is this all about and why did I have to come all the way to New York?"

"Well, there is something important I have to discuss with you," Boris said. "I wanted to discuss it in person, not on the phone or through an e-mail."

Rider released his dick and stood up. He followed Boris to his desk and said, "What is it? Just tell me."

Boris sat down behind his desk and said, "We're going to close the West Hollywood office."

Rider felt a pain in his stomach. "You're joking?"

"I'm afraid not," Boris said. "The world is changing, and things were a lot different when we opened up out there. Gay marriage was still illegal and you did a great job focusing on that and all the controversy that surrounded it. Everything is changing. Gay bars are closing and gay people are assimilating more and more these days. I'm afraid I don't have any other choice but to take things in another direction. Rainbow Palm Productions has to evolve. It has to be more diversified."

Rider turned and glanced out the window. He couldn't say he was totally shocked at hearing all this. He'd noticed the changes in gay culture, too. He'd gone out to the West Hollywood office to head up an LGBTQ web site that focused on news and important issues that affected the LGBTQ community, the most important of which had been legalizing same sex marriage at the time. He'd traveled the country, and the world, focusing on one thing in particular: getting same sex marriage legalized in the US. After the SCOTUS ruling on same sex marriage, his readership didn't seem as interested anymore. Although Rider knew there were still many battles to win, nothing else seemed as important to his readers as legalized marriage had.

"There must be something else we can focus on," Rider said. "You and I both know that there's still as much discrimination and homophobia as there ever was. I won't even begin to get into the passive aggressive homophobia. The one thing different now is that gay marriage is legal. Everything else is still the same."

Boris shrugged and said, "I agree with you. We're working on several new indie films and two documentaries that deal with discrimination. But I have to keep things interesting for the readers if I'm going to keep the Rainbow Palm Productions online content relevant. If you're going to compete nowadays it's all about the clickbait."

Rider turned and faced the other side of the room. "So you're telling me that I'm fired, that I'm out of a job."

"You must have other prospects," Boris said.

"Not one. I've dedicated my life to this company."

"How's your financial situation?"

"Not as good as *yours*," Rider said.

"I see," Boris said. He stood up and started pacing the office. "There is something you might be interested in, but I'm not sure you're the right person for the job. I probably shouldn't even mention it. It's a silly idea."

"What is it?"

Boris walked over to him and said, "Rainbow Palm Productions is going to launch a brand new web site on the West Coast called *Evil Wobniar* ...it's rainbow and live spelled backward."

"How adorable," Rider said, with a sarcastic tone, this time rolling his eyes so hard he almost tipped sideways. "But I don't understand."

"Don't judge it yet," Boris said. "At least not until you've heard more about it. People like that sort of thing these days. They go for cute and they all want something that gives them the feels. Just look at *Etsy* and some of those other web sites with quirky names. People want to be entertained, especially younger people like you."

Rider sighed and asked, "And what's the focus going to be." He'd been focusing on only hard news stories up until then, mainly about equal rights and discrimination.

"Everything," Boris said. "There is no specific focus this time. We're combining news stories with fitness features, healthy recipes with religious discrimination stories. We want this to be a diversified web site for LGBTQ people around the world, where they can scroll down and pick and choose what interests them the most. And, of course, there will be the obligatory features about gay sex."

Rider laughed. "Well, of course. What would a web site geared toward gay men be without sex? Let me guess. A lot of this sex will be about sex with straight men."

Boris walked to the window. "Well, there will be some of that, but that's not all there is to it. As I said, there's no set focus. We're even going to get into gay family pieces and health related articles that focus on things like *PrEP*."

Rider smiled. "But the sex is what will keep them all coming back. Level with me, Boris. I know this business well."

"You don't have to sound so judgmental about it."

Rider rolled his eyes again. "Will there be articles about *awesome* kitty cats and *epic* puppy dogs, because you know how much I love pieces about kitties and puppies?"

"Only when someone eats one."

12

"Well, at least there's *some* hope."

Boris turned and walked over to him again. He put his arm around Rider and guided him over to a sofa near the fireplace. As they sat down, Boris buried his face in Rider's neck and kissed him. When he stopped kissing, he lifted his head and said, "I want you to head this web site up with someone. You'll both be in charge of all the content."

Rider inhaled Boris's scent and ran his palm all the way down his torso. He still smelled of the men's body wash he'd showered with that morning. Rider had forgotten how much he missed having such uncomplicated sex with a man like Boris. "Who is the other person I'll be working with?" He hadn't planned on turning this meeting into a make out session with Boris, but now that he was on the sofa with him he couldn't seem to keep his hands at his sides. He started to wonder if Boris was wearing his usual boxer shorts.

As Rider opened one of the buttons on Boris's dress shirt and slid his hand inside to rub his chest, Boris spread his legs wider and said, "Drew Reinhart."

Rider jumped up from the sofa and said, "*Drew Reinhart.*"

Boris stood up and adjusted his erection. It was poking through his pants and he couldn't hide it. "Yes."

"I've heard enough."

"I want you to listen to everything. Drew is the best editor there is, and you're the best writer there is. No one can work with Drew the way you can. Drew has a knack for clickbait pieces, and you have knack for serious news stories. You'll be the perfect balance and I'm going to need you to keep Drew under control. Drew will deal with the editorial things and the tech issues that come up, and you'll both have a staff working with you. If you need them, we'll even hire more people."

"I have a feeling this was all planned," Rider said. "You wanted me to do this all along and that's why you wanted to see me in person. You set me up because you know how to play me."

Boris shrugged and moved his erection to the right. "Well, it did cross my mind. But you know that I'd never do anything that's not in your best interest. You also know that I do care about you. And I think this is in your best interest. I think it will be a challenge and something that will help you grow professionally. Whether you like it or not, you need to evolve."

Rider started pacing the room. The mention of Drew Reinhart's name turned his nerves raw. They'd been full time lovers and it hadn't been an amicable break up. "You know my history with Drew. We were almost engaged. I'm not sure we can work with each other. The man came after me with a baseball bat once. A person doesn't forget a thing like that."

"From what I've heard, you deserved it. He caught you with the pizza man and the plumber, at the same time, tag teaming you on a table. How clichéd is *that*?"

"Maybe I did deserve it," Rider said. "I'm not perfect and I never said I was. Drew knew that."

"Dude, think about that. The guy came home and found you naked, on your back, with your legs up, getting tag teamed by two guys. What on earth were you thinking?"

"It's not my fault the pizza arrived at the same time the plumber was leaving," Rider said. "And they started it."

"You were walking around in nothing but your underpants."

"It was hot outside."

"I'm not taking sides," Boris said. "I'm just saying that Drew might have had his reasons for getting upset."

"All the more reason why I don't think this arrangement you want us to do will work. He's got a very bad temper."

"I'm only asking you to give it a try," Boris said.

"Does Drew know that I'm going to be working with him?" Rider asked. He hadn't actually spoken to Drew since they'd split up. Drew was in charge of another web site that was part of Rainbow Palm Productions in San Francisco that published mostly clickbait stories about sex, dating, and travel. They used words like *cerulean* instead of just saying blue in that way amateurs tend to exaggerate.

"Yes," Boris said. "I've spoken with him."

"How did he react?"

"The same way you're reacting right now," Boris said. "Then he calmed down and offered to pay for the wall he punched. Now he's looking forward to working with you."

"Somehow I find that hard to imagine…that he's looking forward to it."

"He's willing to give it a try," Boris said. "He's been very professional about it. He understands that I have to consolidate both of these web sites and create a new one, and in one location."

Rider flung him a look and asked, "How much of a raise will I get?" He wasn't about to even consider this offer unless he knew the money was going to be spectacular.

Boris quoted a few numbers and said, "That's the best I can do."

Rider shook his head and said, "Well you'll have to do a lot better if you want me to work with Drew again. Double those numbers and you've got a deal, and I get my own weekly column and byline on the web site, without any censorship at all. I have full control over that particular content." He figured if he was going to do this he might as well try to get more web presence. He'd always wanted his own regular weekly column.

"Okay," Boris said. "It's a deal."

"Really?" He hadn't expected Boris to cave in that quickly.

"Yes, I'm serious. Now come over here and we'll shake on it."

"If I come over there you're going to want more than a handshake," He glanced down at Boris's crotch and pointed to his erection. "It's sticking right out through your pants."

"Well, we haven't seen each other in a while. Come over here and be a good friend."

If this had been anyone else, Rider would have left the office at that moment. With anyone else, it might have implied that he'd gotten his new job because of his cock sucking skills. But with Boris that wasn't the case and he knew it. They'd started having sex long before they'd worked together. He could have left the office at that moment and Boris still would have given him the job and the raise with no bitter feelings.

Rider walked over to where he was standing and said, "Sit down on the couch. And just so you know, I'm only doing this because I want to do it, not because you want me to do it. There's a difference."

Boris hiked up his pant legs, sat down, and spread his legs wide. "I know that, buddy. No worries, man. I know what you like."

"Don't be so smug." Sometimes Rider thought Boris knew him too well.

"Well, you do like it. And I like when you do it. Everyone is happy."

Rider sat down beside him and reached over to pull down his zipper. He knew all Boris wanted to do was sit back, put his hands behind his head, and spread his legs. This was fine with Rider because all he wanted to do was lean over, pull out Boris's dick, and get him off. Boris didn't have a huge dick, and he'd never been big on reciprocation. Most people would have considered him a boring lover. However, there was something about Boris's apathy that set off every dirty, sexual fantasy Rider had ever had about servicing a man this way that he never could resist. At that particular moment, Rider didn't want or need a blow job.

He didn't need to climax either. The only thing he wanted to do at that moment was get Boris off.

A few minutes later, Boris removed his palm from the back of Rider's head and stood up. "Thanks, buddy. That was fantastic, as usual."

While Boris put his dick back into his pants and pulled up his zipper, Rider wiped his lips with the side of his hand and said, "Now my lips will be swollen for the next two hours. I shouldn't have done that. Adults don't blow their bosses in business meetings." He always hated feeling so guilty afterward.

"Don't look at it that way," Boris said. "When you're going down on me I'm not your boss. Think of it as helping out a friend in need."

Rider stood up and shrugged. "Well, only for you. But just so we aren't confused. I can't promise you that this is going to work out with Drew Reinhart. I don't know what to expect, or if we can even work together."

Boris walked over to him and put his arm around him. He kissed him, and then said, "I'm only asking you to give it a try. I think it will be good. Plus, look at all the money you'll be making and you're getting your own weekly column. I think this will help you grow, and you'll have complete creative control. It might even lead to more exposure like a radio show of your own. I plan to constantly expand the media communications department. What more could you want?"

Rider rested him palm on Boris's stomach and said, "Well, you could walk me downstairs. I would like that. I've really missed you a lot and it's the least you could do. I'm heading back to LA tomorrow and we won't see each other again for a time."

Boris rested his hand on the small of Rider's back and guided him to the door. "I was going to walk you down anyway. You didn't have to ask."

Before they reached the door, Rider asked, "I'm curious. Have you ever slept with Drew Reinhart? It's not a big thing. I'm just curious."

"Of course not," Boris said. "I absolutely do *not* sleep with anyone else who works here. You should know that. Besides, he's not my type."

"Okay, I was just curious," Rider said. "Not that it would have mattered. I have no right to even ask that. I'm sorry."

"You now it's times like this I always wonder why we never got together as a couple," Boris said.

"Because we're such good friends, that's why. We don't want to ruin that friendship." He knew Boris would understand what he meant by this. No one else in the world would understand, but they did and that was all that mattered.

CHAPTER TWO

The West Hollywood office that Boris was closing had always been the smallest physical location for Rainbow Palm Productions. It had been located atop a dry cleaning establishment, in between a Chinese take-out and a professional palm reader. Before Rainbow Palm Productions acquired it, the space had been used for a small time private investigator that chased married cheaters and disability frauds around Los Angeles. The physical space consisted of a small reception area and two small back offices that overlooked an alleyway. Even though the majority of all of the hard news stories Rider had ever covered came from that location, Rider was not going to miss the cramped bathroom, or the back fire escape that was the only way to get up there.

When he pulled into the newest West Coast location for Rainbow Palm Productions, he stopped in the middle of a pristine Beverly Hills

---

parking lot surrounded by tall palm trees and glanced at the white building. He found it ironic that his old office had been so dreadful and he'd been working on serious hardcore news. In the same respect, it was the first time he'd ever worked in a building this grand, with free parking and landscaped grounds. He wondered what his office would be like and what his first assignment would be. Most of all, he wondered what it would be like seeing Drew after such a long time.

He parked his black Jeep Wrangler between a silver Mercedes and blue BMW. He made sure he parked straight, within the boundaries of the white lines. He didn't want to piss anyone off on his first day there. As he climbed out of the car and headed toward the building, he straightened his light gray suit jacket and smoothed out his pants. He'd chosen to wear one of his new skinny suits that morning and he wasn't used to the tight pants and short jacket sleeves. The salesperson had told him it was the latest design but he still couldn't help feeling a little like Pee-Wee Herman…along with the urge to giggle aloud.

He entered the lobby and crossed to the elevator. The interior of the building had the same antiseptic feel as a New York skyscraper, with stark white walls and dark brown tiles. He pressed the elevator button a few times and glanced at a directory that said *Wobnair Evil* was located on

23

the top floor. He was a little stunned to see the name of the web site already on the directory, because that meant Boris had been planning this a lot longer than he'd admitted. This didn't bother Rider. In fact, it made him smile to think about Boris trying to figure out ways to get Rider to work there. Even though Rider preferred working on hardcore news stories that had an impact on the LGBT community and humanity, he'd been so focused on nothing but hardcore pieces he was secretly looking forward to doing something lighter and more creative for a change.

When he stepped out of the elevator on the top floor, he turned left and saw *Wobnair Evil* was the first door on the right. The name still made him want to roll his eyes and groan and he was determined to figure out a way to change the name. It wasn't something he would have chosen.

He entered the reception area and found no one sitting behind the main desk. There were a few other smaller desks that lined both sides of the room and they were empty as well. To his left he saw a door with his name on it, and to the right he saw a door with a name plate that read, "Drew Reinhart." Instead of knocking, he opened Drew's door slowly without making a sound and found Drew sitting behind his desk staring down at a keyboard.

Rider stepped into the office and cleared his throat. Drew continued to stare at the keyboard and said, "Did you get that attachment I sent this morning, Dequinn?"

Drew sounded so calm and peaceful Rider almost backed out of the office. Drew hadn't seen him since the day he'd been caught screwing around with the pizza guy and the plumber and he started having second thoughts about this working arrangement. Even he couldn't believe he'd been so wrong to cheat on Drew that way.

He'd already agreed to take the job and he was in no position to turn down the money, so he took another step inside, cleared his throat, and said, "You're looking well, Drew. It's been a long time."

Drew stopped moving his fingers and stared at the keyboard. Then he lifted his head and turned around so abruptly Rider took a step back. He glared at Rider for a moment without saying a word. After he took a deep breath and exhaled, he smiled. "Well, I've been waiting for you to arrive. I see you still haven't learned how to knock on someone's door before entering. From now on, you never come in here without knocking first. Is that understood?"

Although he still sounded calm and affable, Rider noticed the sarcasm and said, "Don't I even get a hello and how are you doing, first?"

Drew smiled and folded his arms across his chest. "You're lucky I don't pick up the first thing I see and hurl it across the room at your pretty little face."

Rider didn't want to sound defensive, so he overcompensated by trying to joke around. "Go ahead. Take your best shot. I won't even move. Just throw whatever you want and I'll stand still and take it."

"Don't be an idiot," Drew said. He'd stopped glaring, but one eyebrow was still higher than the other.

Rider walked over to his desk and said, "You really are looking well, Drew." His honey colored hair was shorter on the sides and longer on the top, his chest muscles rounded through the white V-neck shirt he was wearing, and he had just enough of a tan to give his skin a soft glow. It appeared as if he was beginning to grow a beard, which gave him a rugged appeal that sent a thrill up Rider's leg.

Drew shrugged as if he didn't care and said, "You look the same as always."

"Thank you," Rider said. "You always knew how to pay the best compliments." He'd been trying not to be sarcastic, but that one was too easy to pass. In the short time they were together as a couple if Drew even noticed how Rider looked it was a novelty.

"And you were always so needy," Drew said.

"Now that's not true and you know it," Rider said. He didn't want to start an argument. He'd only been there a few minutes. However, he wasn't going to let Drew get away with that superior tone, especially now that they would be working together on a regular basis.

Drew stood up and turned to glance out the window. His faded jeans were as tight at his shirt and they hugged his slim hips so perfectly Rider felt like walking over and grabbing him.

"You always did need extra attention," Drew said. "If everyone in the room wasn't falling all over you, you worked them even harder until they did."

"Maybe that's because I never got any attention from you," Rider said. He didn't feel like explaining it to Drew, but he had changed in that respect. The older he got the less he seemed to care about what people thought.

"Well, you made up for it. I'll never forget just how much attention you were getting from the pizza delivery guy and the plumber on *that* afternoon."

"Why do you have to bring that up again?" Rider asked. "That's ancient history."

Drew turned and laughed in his face. "You're right. You can't help it if you have needs. The kind of needs that could never be satisfied by one man alone. It's just part of your nature."

"Don't slut shame *me*," Rider said.

"It's not slut shaming when you're talking about your own lover, the person you thought you were in a monogamous relationship with. That's called honesty, and it's something with which you've never been completely familiar."

He had a point and Rider knew it. When he'd seduced the plumber and the pizza guy in his underwear that afternoon he knew he was wrong, and yet he still couldn't keep from doing it. "I'm sorry. I was an idiot."

Drew walked to the other end of the window and glanced out to the parking lot. "It's all good now," he said. "There's no need to apologize. We're both adults and enough time has passed since all that happened. In a way, you actually helped me grow up and face the world as it is." He turned and looked him in the eye. "If anything, I should be thanking you for teaching me a good lesson in life. If it looks too good to be true, it probably is."

He sounded so friendly and calm Rider didn't want to ruin the moment by continuing this conversation. He had a feeling that if he said the wrong thing…which he tended to do…the conversation might devolve into a loud shouting match.

He walked over to the window where Drew was standing and extended his right hand. "Let's start fresh, right now. We're going to be working together, we both want this web site to be successful, and I think we're going to work well together. Let's shake on it, and I'll take you out to dinner tonight to talk everything over."

For a moment, Drew hesitated. When he did finally reach for Rider's hand he shook it and said, "That sounds like a good idea, a business dinner."

"Don't I at least get a hug?" Rider asked.

Drew stepped back and smiled. "Don't push your luck, pal."

Rider smiled and lifted his palms. "Okay."

"Now I have to get back to work, and you need to get set up in your office," Drew said. "If you need anything ask Dequinn. He's kind of like the receptionist, the office manager, and the one who does all the tech work around here. Sandler, who is also on staff, does some tech work, but it's mostly Dequinn."

As Rider turned to leave, he said, "Sounds good. I'll make a reservation somewhere and meet you here in your office at the end of the day."

When Rider reached the door, Drew said, "One more thing. You don't have to dress that way for work."

Rider stopped at the door and turned around. "What's wrong with the way I'm dressed?" He thought he looked great.

Drew looked him up and down and smiled. "It's just that we're more casual here on a daily basis, and you look as if you're going to the first holy communion of the child of a hipster couple. But you always were very trendy."

"Well I'm glad I left my lumberjack beard and fake man bun at home," Rider said. "I'll remember that." No one could throw shade better than Drew, but no one could reply faster than Rider.

"I'm sure you will," Drew said, and then he sat down behind his desk, went back to his keyboard, and dismissed Rider as if he'd already left the room.

When Rider was out in the reception area again, he noticed a nice looking young guy sitting at the main desk. Even though he was seated, he appeared to be taller than most men. He was dressed casually in a white button down shirt and tan jeans, and his short dark hair had a little

extra style to it that was hard to explain. At a glance, he reminded Rider

of a news anchor on one of the large cable news stations, but he had an

edge that resembled a well-known openly gay rap singer. Rider figured

this was Dequinn, so he headed over to introduce himself, wondering

whether or not this unusual working arrangement with Drew would ever

settle into something comfortable.

CHAPTER THREE

During dinner that night, Rider and Drew spent most of their time discussing *Wobnair Evil.* Not the web site content or design, the actual name that Boris had chosen.

"I worry with that name no one will know what it is," Drew said.

"I don't think search engines will even pick it up," Rider said. "Plus, it sucks."

"It's hard enough to get LGBTQ people to read gay news web sites, let alone get anyone in the mainstream to read them. And with a name like *Wobnair Evil* we might be setting ourselves up for failure before we even launch."

"I think we should think about other names," Rider said. "We can present them to Boris tomorrow morning and try to persuade him. I don't want this web site to be something that disappears, and there's going to be competition out there. It's one thing to be trendy and have an unusual name, but we have to be practical, too."

They both agreed they didn't like the name, and then spent the next hour brainstorming for new names. By the time they finished spouting off some of the most ridiculous names on the Internet, Drew suggested they think about it overnight and start fresh again in the morning. He mentioned he'd called a meeting the next morning to discuss the first main feature for the web site. Along with other daily news items that would focus mostly on the lighter side of gay news…the sex-concentrated clickbait articles…they wanted to feature one main story every month that would keep the web site anchored and give them more credibility.

After he finished his third martini, Drew sat back and glanced at Rider from the other side of the table. "Just why are you doing this?"

Rider was still working on his first martini. He'd never been a drinker, and couldn't even handle one martini. He shrugged and said, "I wanted something different."

"Boris didn't give you a choice."

"Well that, too."

"But this web site is going to be mostly garbage for the most part," Drew said. "You've always been so focused on the serious issues like same sex marriage and politics. I've read all of your pieces and I've always admired your ability to focus and remain objective. I hate to say this, but you're too good for this web site."

"You've read everything I've done?" This was news to Rider. He hadn't even read all of his own stories. After he submitted a story for publication, he usually moved on to the next story without even reading what they published.

Drew nodded. "Of course I have. I've read everything from the coverage of gay marriage you did in Washington when the Supreme Court ruled, to the pieces you did in Africa about gay life there. I've always been impressed, if not a little jealous."

"Jealous?"

"Well, not jealous," Drew said. "More like disappointed in myself. I've never had the kind of passion you have for serious hardcore news. This new web site is perfect for me. I don't mind covering clickbait pieces and I'm good at it, but you're so much more serious than I am in that respect. Why are you here, and why would you settle for something like this?"

Rider sat back and shrugged. "I really did want something different, is all. And I couldn't turn down the money. I'm getting paid a lot more now than I ever did in my life. I'm also getting my first regular weekly column. But most of all, I wanted to work with you."

"You're full of crap and you know it," Drew said. "You're probably more interested in the weekly column than anything."

Rider laughed. "Well you can believe what you want, but I did want to work with you. We're good together. We balance each other. And I think we have unsettled business."

Drew thought about that for a moment, and then stood up and said, "It's late and we both have to get up early."

"We do?"

Drew nodded. "Yes, I've already said that I called a meeting first thing in the morning in my office so we can discuss the new feature with the staff and make plans. I even sent you an e-mail about it. If you'd read your e-mails you'd have known this."

"Oh, e-mail," Rider said. "I have to get used to using that again. I'm so used to texting I overlook it sometimes."

Drew reached into his pocket for his wallet and said, "As I recall, you weren't good at returning texts either."

Rider knew he was right so he changed the subject fast. He stood up and said, "I'm paying. This dinner is on me."

"Calm yourself," Drew said. "Boris is paying. This was a business dinner and I'm writing it off as an expense."

A few minutes later when they climbed into Rider's Jeep, Drew told Rider to bring him back to the office so he could pick up his car and Rider refused. He thought Drew had had too much to drink and he didn't want him to drive. Even though Drew appeared to be sober, Rider didn't want him taking any chances. Rider barely had one drink, and he'd nursed it all evening. He was also curious about where Drew was living. Up until recently, the last he'd heard Drew had been living in San Francisco, mostly working out of a home office for Rainbow Palm Productions in San Francisco. After they closed the San Francisco office and the West Hollywood office to open the new one in Beverly Hills, Drew had moved to LA indefinitely.

They pulled up to a craftsman style bungalow in West Hollywood that was sandwiched in between a large mid-century modern affair and a gigantic Mediterranean villa. Even though it was small, it competed with charm without even trying too hard. The exterior was pale sage green with bright white trim, had a large front porch with two swings, a brick front walk, and perfectly manicured hedgerows. It looked more like it should have been in Seattle than West Hollywood.

As they headed up the brick path, Rider said, "Where did you find a place like this? I've been living in WeHo for a few years and I'm renting a dismal studio apartment from two closeted gay guys who are renting a house. This looks like something out of a fairytale, with secret gardens and magical butterflies."

Drew smiled. "I like it a lot. I'm renting it through a friend of Boris's who will be working in Asia for the next three years. I got lucky. All I had to do was unpack my suitcases."

When they reached the front door and Drew unlocked it, Rider tried to step inside first but Drew blocked the entrance with his arm.

"I thought you would at least offer me a nightcap," Rider said. They were standing face to face, only inches apart, eye to eye. He gave Drew a more seductive glance and ran his hand up Drew's other arm.

"I have to get up early," Drew said. "And so do you."

Rider ignored him and ducked under the arm that was blocking the doorway. He walked into the main living space of Drew's house and stood there with his hands in his pockets looking around while Drew closed the door.

"This is as nice on the inside as it is on the outside," Rider said. "It has a comfortable, homey appeal." The room was decorated in several shades of beige, with red leather club chairs and a dark brown leather sofa that had been weathered in purpose. The hand crafted Middle Eastern rugs added most of the color to the room, and a few abstract paintings with simple black frames kept it from looking too much like a crafty knitting grandma's house. It had a trendy edge that reminded Rider of a New York coffee house in SoHo. "This is exactly the kind of place I would imagine you living in, Drew."

"I like it," Drew said. He flipped on a main switch that illuminated every lamp in the room, and then set his keys on a table near the door and crossed to a mission style cabinet next to the fireplace. "What would you like?"

"A little port would be nice. I'll sip it."

Drew almost smiled, but stopped. Drew already knew that port made Rider horny…Rider had mentioned this many times…but he didn't acknowledge it aloud. "I'm all out of port."

"Then I'll have whatever you're having."

While Drew poured the drinks, Rider walked around the living room and pretended to check out the paintings. He only had one thing on his mind that night and he couldn't have cared less what was hanging on the walls. And when Drew sat down on the sofa a few minutes later and set the drink on the coffee table, Rider sat down next to him and said, "I bet your bedroom is just as nice as this room."

Drew sipped his drink and said, "It's very nice. I like it."

Although Rider couldn't be certain about whether or not Drew wanted to sleep with him again, he moved a little closer and rested his palm on Drew's thigh. He rubbed his thigh a few times and said, "I'd love to see it."

Drew pointed to a hallway on the other side of the room and said, "If you'd like to go in and look, feel free. But I'll wait here." Then he reached down, lifted Rider's hand from his thigh, and set it on Rider's lap.

"You're still mad at me," Rider said. "You said you weren't mad anymore, but I can tell."

"I don't know what you're talking about."

"Oh yes you do," Rider said. "I know you too well."

"No one has ever hurt me the way you did," Drew said. He finished his drink and slammed the glass on the coffee table. "I thought we were in a relationship. I thought we were serious about each other. I thought we would spend the rest of our lives together…until I walked in that day and found the pizza guy and the plumber fucking your brains out on the dining room table."

"I've apologized for that a million times," Rider said. "I was wrong. I hated myself just as much as you hated me. But there's something I didn't tell you, something I didn't even realize myself until after I'd done what I did. I was scared. We'd both just graduated from college and I wasn't ready for anything that serious. And I loved you so much I couldn't say no to anything. I even agreed when you said you wanted to adopt kids and start a family. I don't even know if I like kids. And while I was saying yes, I was getting this pain in my stomach the whole time."

"You were lying to me?" Drew asked.

"No," Rider said. "Well, not lying in a bad way. I was agreeing with you because I didn't have the heart to say no. I loved you so much I would have done anything to please you, and that scared me to death."

"So you slept with other people instead of telling me how you really felt," Drew said. "What a novel way to show love."

"I didn't do it on purpose," Rider said. "I just wasn't ready for that kind of a commitment and I didn't know how to tell you. I didn't want to hurt you. I didn't plan on you walking in that day. I didn't think you'd be home until much later."

When Drew saw that Rider was telling him the truth, his expression softened and he hesitated before he replied. "It wasn't like I was forcing you to get married at gunpoint."

Rider chose his words with care. "You did have a china pattern picked out at Williams Sonoma."

"I guess I misunderstood," Drew said. "I thought we were moving forward. I had no idea you wanted to get out of the relationship so much."

"I didn't want to get out of the relationship totally," Rider said. "I just wanted a little more freedom and to slow things down. And you were always so nice I didn't want to hurt your feelings."

Drew stood up and crossed to the fireplace. "I see."

"You *do?*"

"I think so," Drew said. Then he walked slowly back to the sofa, stood in front of Rider, and pulled down his zipper. "Give me a blowie."

"*Huh?*"

He whipped his dick out of his pants and leaned forward. "I said give me a blowie."

Rider nearly dropped his drink. "I thought you had to get up early."

"This won't take long."

Rider stared at Drew's dick and gulped. It was hanging out of his jeans and semi-erect. In the past when they'd made love, Rider had always been the one to make the first move.

"Is this a trick?" Rider asked. He'd never heard Drew speak this way before, or with this aggressive tone. His heart started to race and the room felt warmer.

"Just do it and shut up."

Rider took a quick breath and leaned forward. He rested one hand on Drew's thigh and grabbed his dick with the other. It was almost fully erect by then, well over eight inches in length and thick enough to be more than a handful at the base. When he opened his mouth and slid Drew's dick along his tongue, he looked up and Drew said, "That's it, look up at me with those big brown eyes while you suck. I like that."

Although Rider wasn't sure what had brought about this sudden change in Drew, he started sucking that dick as if he hadn't sucked dick in years. While he sucked, Drew pulled off his shirt and threw it across the room. His chest was bigger than Rider remembered and his stomach muscles even more defined. He'd been working out regularly, to the point where he'd reached an almost perfect body. However, as Drew held his head and fucked his face, Rider remembered his scent most of all. He hadn't showered since early that morning and the familiar scent of his crotch was stronger. And even though there was no way to compare it to anything, the smell of him flung Rider back to the days when they'd first met in college.

At one point, Drew held Rider's head and pulled his dick out of his mouth. When Rider looked up at him to see what was wrong, Drew smiled and said, "Get naked," and then he pushed Rider's head back with force and began to remove his own jeans.

While Drew stripped naked, Rider removed his clothes so fast he knocked a lamp off a table next to the sofa. He moved with such alacrity he thought his hands might start to shake. He couldn't believe this was actually happening. He'd been prepared for Drew to have a quick drink and show him the door. And now that this was happening, he wanted it more than he had when he'd entered Drew's house.

When Rider was naked, he stood up to head into Drew's bedroom. That's the way they'd always made love when they'd been a couple. They'd always done it in bed, under the covers, in the dark, without surprises. The few times Rider had suggested they make love in other places, Drew always shot him down. Drew claimed it was more romantic and intimate in the bedroom and Rider always agreed because he didn't want to disappoint him or hurt his feelings. He'd always been so careful to do and say things with which Drew would agree.

As Rider stood up, Drew grabbed him by the neck and said, "Turn around and spread your legs."

Rider froze. He looked up at him in disbelief. "Right here? In the living room?"

"I said turn around."

As Rider turned around to face the back of the sofa, Drew grabbed the boxer briefs he'd been wearing all day and he shoved them up against Rider's face and held them there for a moment. He'd never done *anything* like this before with his underpants, but Rider didn't complain. They smelled good; he inhaled deeply. And he continued turning until he could grab the back of the sofa for support.

When Rider spread his legs and arched his back, Drew pulled the boxer briefs over his head to cover Rider's face.

He knew he was about to get fucked by Drew and he couldn't spread his legs wide enough. But he also said, "Only with a condom."

Drew patted the bottom of his ass a couple of times and said, "Yeah, I've got that covered, so to speak."

Although Rider couldn't see a thing with Drew's underpants over his head, he heard Drew moving around, and a minute later he felt Drew's fingers at the lips of his anus. Evidently, Drew kept condoms and lube in the living room, which he'd never done when they'd been a couple. It didn't matter at that point. Drew's middle finger entered him slowly, a second finger probed him for a few minutes, and then he pulled his fingers out and shoved his dick into Rider's body so hard Rider went forward until he was pinned against the back of the sofa. It felt wonderful and familiar, and yet odd and unexpected at the same time. The entire experience left Rider between ecstasy and wondering what in the world was happening to him.

Drew took him with such force that night the narrow table behind the sofa fell over sideways. He held Rider's waist and pounded with such a steady even pace Rider almost started begging him to continue. Of course he didn't do that. He didn't want Drew to think he was having too much fun, so he remained speechless, on purpose. He didn't want to ruin the moment either. Rider had been around and he'd been with so many men by then he'd lost count and Drew had a tendency to slut shame him. Drew did this in a sarcastic way…most of the time…but it still bothered Rider, and that's mainly because Drew always seemed to expect so much from him. Rider had always been the first to admit he was only human and as imperfect as anyone could possibly be. Even though it wasn't always the best reason, it was the truth.

As he lost track of everything, Rider felt as if he'd been thrust into the middle of a gay porn video, where nothing else mattered but reaching a climax at the end. In the same respect, even this sex with Drew was still tame compared to other men Rider had taken. There was no vulgar dirty talk and Rider held back with Drew in way he wouldn't have with other men. It didn't take long; Drew started to grunt and pound harder. By the time Drew's body went dead still, and he was in Rider as deeply as he could get, Rider reached down to grab his own dick and they came several seconds apart.

A moment after that, Drew held his waist and guided him face down onto the sofa. As Drew rested on top of him, still deep inside, Rider pushed the black boxer briefs up above his forehead and said, "Let's sleep like this, right here, all night." He chose his words with care; he didn't want to sound like a slut.

Drew kissed the back of his neck and said, "I thought it was nice. You're still as tight as you always were. You're a good lay and always so willing to submit to a guy."

Rider laughed. "Well that's not the most romantic thing to say." He wanted Drew to put his arms around him so they could fall asleep that way. Was that too much to expect, especially with someone who shared a history with him?

Without warning, Drew stood up fast and said, "What just happened between us wasn't about romance, baby. You got what you needed and I got what I wanted." Then he slapped Rider's ass and said, "And now it's time for you to go home and for me to go to bed."

At first, Rider thought he was joking. Drew had always been the one who wanted to cuddle after sex. He turned and sent him a backward glance. "You want me to go home? Right now?"

Drew still had the condom on his dick. He reached out, pulled the underwear off Rider's head, and said, "As cute as you look with my underpants on your head, I think you'd better take them off when you're driving home."

Well.

Drew tossed his underpants on the floor and reached down to pull the condom off his dick. "C'mon, man. You'd better get dressed. It's really getting late."

When Rider realized Drew was serious, he stood up and walked around the living room looking for his clothes. He wasn't totally sure what had just happened between them and he was too confused to ask. Even though they'd just made love, he had a feeling things between them still weren't perfect. And he still had to work with Drew the next morning, so he figured the less he said the better. One of Rider's best traits had always been that he knew how clueless he could be at times and he knew when to keep his mouth shut.

He wanted to say something, or ask Drew a few questions, but it didn't matter much anyway. The next thing Rider knew he was dressed and Drew was leading him toward the front door with his hand pressed hard against the small of his back.

Drew opened the door for him and said, "I'll see you in the morning."

Rider nodded. "Don't I at least get a kiss goodbye?"

Drew leaned forward and gave him a quick peck on the cheek. "There you are. Now drive safely."

"Okay," Rider said. "I don't want to ask too many questions, but what just happened here was a good thing? Right?"

"I enjoyed it," Drew said. "Did you?"

"Or course I enjoyed it," Rider said. "I'm just curious about what this was all about. You've never been like that before. That spontaneous and aggressive."

"We're two adults who had a good time," Drew said. "We work together, we're familiar, and it was a good fuck. I needed some ass, and you needed a stud tonight. Think of me as a stud."

"This isn't like you, Drew. You've never been this cold and impersonal before."

Drew shrugged and said, "That's because I've changed since the last time you saw me. I'm the one who doesn't want to rush into anything anymore. I'm the one who wants to explore things and take his time. I hope you understand that."

"Do I have a choice?"

"No."

"Well I do understand," Rider said. "And I don't blame you." Then he reached up, put his arms around Drew's shoulders, and kissed him on the mouth. It wasn't a quick peck on the lips this time. Their tongues met and Rider held him so hard he fell against the door.

When they stopped kissing, Rider stepped back and looked him in the eye. "Now *that's* a goodbye kiss."

Drew smiled. "Damn you and your adorable brown eyes."

Rider turned to leave and said, "I'll see you in the morning."

As he headed down the brick walk to the Jeep, he pulled Drew's underpants out of his pocket and put them on his head. He'd shoved them into his pocket while he was getting dressed and Drew wasn't looking.

Drew said, "Drive safely, you little jerk."

Rider glanced back with the underpants on his head, and said, "I love you, too."

CHAPTER FOUR

"I've got the perfect name for the web site," Rider said. "It came to me while I was driving home last night from your place."

"Didn't I mention something to you about knocking whenever you come into my office?" Drew asked. He'd stormed into Drew's office again that morning without knocking. Drew opened a small bottle of aspirin, popped two in his mouth, and swallowed them with a few sips of black coffee.

"You look awful," Rider said. He remembered that Drew was prone to hangovers. Even though he could drink without appearing intoxicated, the side effects the next day included dark circles beneath his eyes, a blank expression, and a mood so dark a long nap couldn't even fix him.

Drew rubbed his temples and said, "I've had better mornings."

Rider sat down on the edge of Drew's desk and said, "Well, at least we have a name for the web site now. Do you want to hear it?"

"Do I have to? Can't it wait until later? I'd just like to get through this meeting."

"*LGBTQlive.com.*"

"He tells me anyway."

"Don't you love it?" Rider asked. "Isn't it perfect?"

"First, how can you be so cheerful this early in the morning? Second, I don't love it. There's already another gay web site with a name similar to that, and you know how I feel about the Q word. I don't mind if other gay people want to be referred to as queer, but I'd rather not be referred to as queer myself. I've spent most of my life fighting pejoratives like that and I'm not about to work with a web site that has that word in it."

"I forgot about that," Rider said. He remembered how Drew used to go off on long rants about being called queer. "We can just drop the Q. It still works without it. But I think we should keep it because a lot of people don't agree with you. The Q can also mean *Questioning*. There are a lot of people who fall under the umbrella of LGBT."

"As I said, there's another web site with a similar name. I'd like something different."

Rider glanced down at his lap and made a face. He should have known better than to offer any suggestions at all. It was obvious that Drew was still mad at him for what had happened a few years ago, and Drew was taking it out on him professionally.

"Oh, dear God please don't sulk. I always hated it when you sulked."

"I'm not sulking," Rider said. "I'm thinking. There's a difference."

Drew rolled his eyes. "No, you're sulking. You're a sulker. I've seen you do that a million times before." He took another sip of coffee, a deep breath, and sighed. "Look, I'm not shooting the idea down for personal reasons. I just want this web site to be slightly different than what's already out there. Something for a new century that's not as subjective as other gay web sites are."

"You don't want to alienate people either," Rider said. "Or insult them. People are still very fragile."

"But that's my point," Drew said. "I've studied and researched every single gay news web site out there and they're all the same. They focus on one type of rhetoric, they usually share the same news stories, and the message is always the same. And whenever I read the reader comments at the end of each story, I see the frustration from so many other gay men who don't feel as if they are being informed in a fair and unbiased manner. I know we can't please everyone, but gay men are a diversified group and I don't even think we've begun to hear from them all. All I'm looking for is diversity. I don't want to insult or turn anyone off. I just want something that's balanced. Kind of like a New York Times for LGBT people. This web site is not only about gay men. As you just stated, this web site is about everyone under the umbrella in the LGBT community."

Rider jumped off the edge of the desk and said, "That's it. That's perfect."

Drew tilted his head to the side. "I don't understand. Please don't shout."

"We can call the web site *The Rainbow Times*," Rider said. "I love it. I love it even more than my idea."

Drew sat back in his chair and thought for a moment. Then he glanced up and said, "You know, it's not bad. I actually like it. *TheRainbowTimes.com*. And it's a lot better than *Wobnair Evil*."

"I even like the short version, TRT," Rider said. "Because you know that's what everyone does. They abbreviate, especially when they tweet."

"Good," Drew said. "Not that that's settled you can call Boris and tell him. But ask Dequinn to do a detailed search first to be sure no one else is using it."

"Why should I call Boris?" Rider knew how much Boris liked the name he'd chosen and he didn't want to be the one to criticize him.

"Because you're the one who sucks his dick," Drew said.

"That's not fair."

"It's true."

"I know, but it's not fair," Rider said. "And there's no reason for you to get jealous or nasty about Boris. You knew about Boris and me from the start. There's never been anything deeper than friendship and sex between us."

"I'm not jealous," Drew said. "I'm simply stating a fact. You've sucked his dick and God knows what else. I think it would be easier coming from you than it would from me. You seem to be able to get away with anything with Boris. I can't."

"Yes, I've sucked his dick and I'm not apologizing for that," Rider said. He didn't appreciate the tone in Drew's voice, or the implications. He knew there was slut-shaming somewhere in his comments and he was doing it in that clever passive aggressive way he had. Drew had always been one of those people who could pay a person a compliment and insult them at the same time and they didn't realize it until an hour later.

"And I hope you enjoyed sucking his dick," Drew said. "I couldn't care less."

Rider's face started to get warm. "Well, for your information I did enjoy sucking his dick. In fact, I sucked his dick in New York last week. He has a *great* dick."

Dequinn walked into the office at the same time Rider finished the sentence about sucking Boris's dick. The poor guy stopped at the door, his eyes opened wide, and he said, "I'm sorry if I'm interrupting. I'll come back in a few minutes."

Drew rolled his eyes again and said, "It's all right, Dequinn. Rider was just telling me about his active love life, as he is always so eager to do with anyone who is willing to listen. What did you want?"

Dequinn glanced at Rider and smiled. His expression suggested eagerness instead of chagrin. Then he looked at Drew and said, "The staff is outside waiting."

"Tell them to come in," Drew said. He glanced at Rider. "We can finish this conversation later."

"I'll look forward to it," Rider said.

A minute later, Dequinn returned with the rest of the staff. As they took seats, Drew and Rider joined them in a small seating area that consisted of a black leather sofa, a rustic coffee table that looked as if it was from restoration hardware, and two matching black leather club chairs. Rider had met everyone the day before through Dequinn so no introductions were necessary.

Rider sat down on the arm of the sofa next to a young woman named Ella, a thin lesbian wearing flat ballerina slippers. She was in her twenties and had short bleached hair with inch long dark roots, which seemed to be on purpose. Dequinn, who was the most important part of the staff because of his tech skills, sat in one club chair and a young guy with dark wavy hair and perpetual five o'clock shadow sat in the other. His name was Sandler and he wore thick black rimmed glasses, skinny jeans, and a tight plaid shirt. He seemed to have a nice bulge in his pants…it moved when he walked…and Rider wondered if he was a top or a bottom. With guys like him it was usually hard to tell. Drew pulled up a side chair and sat on the other side of the coffee table, and a guy named Skip sat down on the other arm of the sofa. Skip was the only one in the group over forty years old and he reminded Rider of an aging circuit boy. He wore tight T-shirts and his body had that beefy, muscular look that suggested he'd done a few steroids in his time.

When they were all seated, Drew said, "This isn't going to be complicated. Ella, Dequinn, and Skip will stay here in New York and keep the office running. You'll continue to do what you've been doing, except for Dequinn. We've come up with a new name for the web site and you'll deal with all that so we're ready to launch on time. I'll go into more detail about that with you later, Dequinn. I still have to get approval from the main office."

Rider cleared his throat. "Yes, we still have to mention it to Boris." He shot Drew a look.

Drew didn't react. He ignored Rider and said, "Rider, Sandler, and I are going to Vermont to cover the first feature story. We leave at the end of the week. The focus of the story will be on two middle aged gay men who run a film studio called *Eagle Studios*. I'm sure you're all familiar with what they produce. If you're not, there's always Google. Their names are Rodney Thornside and Jade Blake."

While the others all exchanged glances, Rider stood up and said, "They do gay porn. That's our first feature? A couple of pornsters?"

Drew looked up at him and remained as calm and organized as ever. "I like to refer to it as adult entertainment. They are a very interesting couple who have been fighting for legalized gay marriage for years, fighting censorship for years, and they've been kind enough to open up their lives for us and we're going to treat them with dignity and respect."

Thatcher started to pace the room. "Didn't they do a feature once with someone about their open relationship?"

Drew looked at him and said, "Yes, among other things. They aren't strangers to the press, as you would assume in this case. However, that was mostly Rodney Thornside promoting their business. Jade Blake has never actually been the focus of anything significant."

"Didn't one of them shoot the other in the foot once, literally, in the foot?" Rider asked.

"Well, yes," Drew said. "But that was an accident and I've promised we won't bring that up at all in the feature. I don't know the details, I'm not going to ask, and I don't really care about them."

When Rider saw the stoic expression on Drew's face, he figured it would be wise to not try to make jokes about this story. But he was curious about something. "Why is our first feature going to be about two middle aged men who make gay porn? Is that really the most appropriate topic for a first feature story? How did you come to this conclusion?"

Drew sat back and said, "Look, I know what you're all thinking. This is going to be just another clickbait piece that exploits gay men and the gay sex stereotypes. Part of that is true. We need something with clickbait appeal to attract people to the web site through random searches. Everyone does it and we have to compete. I'm not looking to break the Internet with our first feature, but I don't want to sit there without any hits either. You can't compete or survive these days without some clickbait. And as the old saying goes, sex does, indeed, sell. However, I can promise you this will be different."

"How will it be different?" Rider asked. He knew he would be doing a lot of fluff pieces but he never assumed the first feature would be this blatant.

Drew sent him a smile. "For one thing, you'll be writing it, Rider. It won't be as poorly written and other gay web sites. It won't be filled with clichés, overused adverbs, and bad puns. And I have no doubt you're going to find the perfect angle. I'll be guiding you and editing it. You'll see. You just have to trust me on this one. It won't be geared toward promoting their porn films and it's *not* an advertorial. This feature has strong possibilities. The focus is on the people, not what they do. I'm hoping you'll all be sympathetic and not judgmental."

"It doesn't bother me," Skip said. "I think it sounds interesting."

"I think it sounds fascinating," Ella said. "I'm looking forward to it."

Sandler smiled. "I'm fine."

Rider sent him a look and said, "Yes you are fine, Sandler." He couldn't stop thinking about the bulge in his skinny jeans. He also knew that remark would irritate Drew and he couldn't resist.

Drew just sighed again and said, "If anyone has any questions at any time, you can either text or e-mail Rider or me."

Rider laughed. "Just not in the middle of the night, folks…and I'm not fond of group texts."

Drew ignored that comment as well and stood up. "Let's get to work. We have a great deal to do before the launch deadline and I want perfection."

Rider followed the rest of them out of the office so he could go back to his office and start working on a few of his new weekly columns. He wanted to be prepared in advance and have at least four columns ready at all times. His first column was focused on gender politics with respect to gay men in gay fiction, a topic he'd seen a few times in scholarly posts and articles, but had never actually explored himself. And, the articles he'd seen had never been done by a gay man. At least his regular weekly column would give him something serious to write about, because in spite of Drew's claims that the first feature would be more than just a sex piece, Rider had some serious doubts that morning about the integrity of entire web site.

CHAPTER FIVE

"Well, we're definitely not in Kansas anymore," Rider said. "You're sure this is still Vermont and we didn't take a wrong turn somewhere?"

"Don't be glib, Rider," Drew said. "It's unbecoming of you. And Sandler, close your mouth or they'll think there's something wrong with you. It's like you've never seen two men having sex outdoors before."

"Actually, I haven't," Sandler said, in a deadpan voice.

Rider smiled. "Really?" He loved that innocent quality Sandler had.

Drew rolled his eyes, and Sandler just shrugged in a defeated way.

The three of them had just arrived at Rodney Thornside and Jade Blake's home in Northern Vermont. They'd flown into Burlington, rented a car, and driven the rest of the way up to the little town of

Ryan Field

Elizabethville, not to be confused with Elizabethtown which was located ten miles to the west. They were so close to the Canadian border Rider had noticed signs for Montreal, and so far from the warmth of West Hollywood Rider kept fighting the urge to shiver. The only thing missing was a moose.

"How can they do that in this weather, you know, what they're doing?" Rider asked. "It's so cold." When no one answered the front door, they walked around to the back of the house because they heard people talking. They had no idea they would stumble upon a gay porn film in the making. However, Rider was staring at two attractive young naked men having anal sex on a large, flat rock, with camera pointed in their direction.

Drew shook his head. "How should I know? Maybe they're acclimated."

"I guess they *are*," Rider said. He pulled his jacket collar up around his face.

Sandler just continued to stare at the two young guys having sex, tilting his head sideways every so often.

"From what I gather, Jade and Thorn got this entire complex at a very good price," Drew said. Drew had been reaching out to them

64

through e-mails and phone calls, and learning the basics about them for the feature. "It was only supposed to be a summer retreat but they liked it up here so much they decided to move their entire business and their lives." He pointed to a newer looking one story building, with white stucco walls and a mansard roof. "That's the studio over there. Jade and Thorn live in the main house where we just knocked on the door."

Rider glanced at Sandler and asked, "Are you okay, man? You look a little frazzled." He'd been gaping at the two guys having sex for so long his eyes had glazed over.

"I'm good," Sandler said.

Drew and Rider exchanged a glance, and Rider asked, "So just what is the focus going to be with this feature? I thought you said it wouldn't be about porn."

"It's not about porn," Drew said. "They're obviously working on a film and we just happened to come along at the same time."

Rider glanced around at the house and the property and asked, "So this is where they live *and* work?"

Drew nodded. "The big red renovated barn with white trim is their residence. It used to be a bed and breakfast, until a large ski resort moved into town and took away all of the bed and breakfast trade here in town. From what I gather, the tourists and skiers all go up to the mountain and stay at the brand new modern hotel there, or they rent condos that are part of the resort. No one stays in town anymore. The bed and breakfasts that are left cater to college students and bargain hunters."

Before Rider had a chance to respond, a tall, thin man in his early forties walked over to them and asked, "May I help you?" He had short salt and pepper hair, a ruddy complexion that suggested he'd seen too much sun in his day, and Diesel jeans that hugged his slim hips and made his crotch bulge out. If it hadn't been for his hair, Rider would have guessed he was still in his thirties.

Drew smiled. He reached out the shake the man's hand. "I'm Drew Reinhart, from the web site that's going to do a feature on you and your partner. It's nice to finally meet you in person." Drew evidently knew who this man was.

"Oh, yes," the man said with a soft spoken voice. "I'm Jade Blake. It's nice to meet you as well. We've been expecting you." He gestured to the rock where the two guys had just finished the anal intercourse scene. They'd both come, the top had pulled out, and the bottom was already standing naked on the grass rubbing his backside. "Thorn is somewhere over there wrapping up this scene."

After Drew introduced Rider and Sandler, Jade shook their hands and said, "It's a pleasure to meet you. We're all looking forward to this feature more than you know. We've been planning our wedding around it."

"Your wedding?" Drew asked.

"Yes," said Jade. "I thought Thorn mentioned it to you. We decided to get legally married." He poked Rider in the ribs and laughed. "We've been living in sin, so to speak, for so long now we decided to make it official and make this the focus of the feature story. And we've been contributing to the cause for many years."

Rider smiled. He sent Drew a glance. "I love it. A happily ever after story." Even though Jade wouldn't get it, he didn't try to hide his sarcasm from Drew.

Drew didn't seem amused. He gave Rider a look, and then smiled at Jade and said, "I think it's a wonderful idea. I'm sure it will be a wonderful wedding and it will be great for the feature. We're all looking forward to it."

In a flat tone, Rider said, "It's what I live for." He couldn't imagine anything more boring than writing about the marriage of two middle aged gay pornsters. He'd been covering the legalization of same sex marriage for the last few years and he'd met quiet, humble gay couples…men and women…who had struggled and sacrificed to see that one spectacular day when their relationships could be validated by the law in the country where they'd lived and paid taxes all of their lives. He'd seen so much love and dedication in the most ordinary places, this feature about two gay men who'd become wealthy through porn seemed unbalanced. He wasn't judging them; he was no saint himself. He was only wondering about what readers might think because there didn't seem to be much of a chance to incorporate anything romantic into this story. This was the problem with the entire feature for Rider. He didn't know how to make it interesting and romantic, which had never happened before.

While Jade was telling them about the wedding plans, Rodney Thornside…Thorn for short…walked over to where they were standing and said, "This must be the crew from that new web site that's launching. Sorry there was no one at the house to welcome you. We're all out back here wrapping up a scene in our newest venture. This film is going to be called, *Give Him a Lift*." Then he tossed his head back and laughed at his own porn film title. He was as thin and well-toned as his partner, Jade, however, he dyed his short hair so dark it looked as if he'd painted his skull with black lacquer.

Rider detected a Texas accent, and he noticed his cowboy boots. "Well now that's a great title, and from what I could see happening on that rock over there, it's appropriate, too." The top guy had been screwing the bottom so hard he actually did lift him up at one point.

Drew ignored Rider and introduced everyone to Thorn. Rider felt awkward shaking Thorn's hand because he'd seen Thorn pat one of the naked actors on the ass, the bottom who had just gotten fucked. He made a mental note to wash his hands as soon as he could find a bathroom.

Thorn looked Sandler up and down. "You're a mighty fine looking young man. Did you ever think of acting? Geek porn is really popular now."

Drew blinked.

Rider's jaw dropped.

Sandler took a step back and said, "*Geek porn.*"

"Yeah, you know, nice looking young guys who wear glasses and love to read books, or the tech types," Thorn said. "You have that look. It's not a bad thing. It's very big these days with amateur films. We're going to start a geek film soon and you might be interested. Are you a top or a bottom?"

"Ah well," Sandler said. He took another step back.

Rider could see that Sandler was too stunned to know how to reply, so he put his palm on the small of Sandler's back and said, "Well, thanks for the offer, but he's got a good position with us at the web site." Although they were only a few years apart in age, there was something more innocent and quiet about Sandler that made Rider want to protect him. It was obvious the poor guy wasn't used to dealing with aggressive types, but Rider had run across Thorn's kind before and he wanted Thorn to know it.

When Thorn raised an eyebrow at Rider's comment, Drew must have sensed the tension. He smiled and said, "It's been a long day and we've been traveling since early this morning. Why don't we go to our rooms and unwind for a while. We left our luggage at the front door."

"That's a good idea," Jade said. "I'll take you into the house while Thorn helps clear up the set out here. There's only one issue, though. We hadn't planned on it, but Thorn's aunt is coming to the wedding from Boston and we had to have a room for her. So we only have two bedrooms for you guys. I hope two of you don't mind sharing one. They're very large rooms."

"Not at all," Rider said. "I'd be happy to share a room with Sandler." He figured he would say it first so Drew wouldn't shoot him down.

"I'm sure you would," Drew said, with a sardonic tone.

"Well, of course if you want to share a room with me, Drew, that's okay, too," Rider said.

"No thanks," Drew said. "I'm good."

"I figured you'd want to have a room all by yourself," Rider said, smiling at Drew. He wanted to see if Drew would get jealous. He smiled at the others and said, "Drew snores."

Drew glared at him as if he wanted to kick him. "You're too thoughtful, Rider. What would I do without you and all of that clever wit?"

Sandler didn't realize there was anything going on between Rider and Drew. He knew nothing of their back story. He just shrugged and said, "I don't mind sharing a room with Rider. It's fine."

Ryan Field

"Then it's all settled," Jade said. "Let's go inside and I'll show you around."

The gigantic, old red and white barn didn't have any distinct style. Even though it had a few Edwardian traits, it reminded Rider of a huge, long converted warehouse. It wasn't exactly barn-shaped with a Dutch colonial roof. They entered a large front hall with white walls and rustic wide plank floors. From what Rider could see at a glance, the white walls and wooden floors continued throughout the first floor of the house. Everything had a quasi-grand, pretentious look, but in a forced minimalist way. It was obvious they were trying hard to keep this place from looking too much like a classic barn and more like a city loft. The few pieces of furniture Rider noticed were either Shaker style or stark mid-century modern. Most of the walls were either void of art, or had an over-sized colorful abstract. And in direct contrast to all of this forced simplicity...or absurdity...there were so many over-sized, ornate crystal chandeliers hanging in unexpected places, Rider found it more whimsical than sophisticated.

Jade led them to a wide staircase in the center of the house, and they followed him up to the second floor. The walls were all white up there as well, and there were even more crystal chandeliers staggered in

72

the most unusual places. The only difference between the first floor and the second appeared to be the flooring. The wide planks were the same upstairs, but instead of being left natural they'd painted them all classic Tiffany blue.

When they passed the first two doors on the left and right, Jade gestured and said, "The one on the right is my bedroom and the one on the left is Thorn's." He sent them a backward glance and smiled. "We haven't shared a bedroom or bathroom in years. It makes for a happier marriage."

"I'm sure it does, especially if one snores," Rider said. This wasn't the first time Rider had heard about this. He'd known more than a few established gay couples who slept in separate bedrooms.

Drew glared at Rider again, and Rider smiled.

When they reached the end of the hall, Thorn gestured to the left and said, "You can have this room, Drew, and Rider and Sandler can have the one across the hall. If you need anything just let me know. We're planning a special dinner tonight at eight o'clock. I hope Thorn's aunt from Boston will be here by then. You never know with *that* one." He laughed. "I stopped trying to figure *her* out years ago."

Rider wanted to ask more about Thorn's aunt, but he had a feeling it was too soon and he didn't want to appear pushy. So he smiled instead and said, "I'm looking forward to meeting her." Actually, he was hoping to find someone relatively interesting.

Jade laughed and turned to head back to the stairs. "No, trust me, you're not looking forward to meeting her. It's just that we can't avoid it this time. Thorn's aunt raised him and he's very close to her. She had to be invited. I'm used to her by now, but strangers usually find her a bit eccentric."

"I see," Drew said. "Well, I'm sure we'll all get along just fine."

When Jade headed back downstairs, Rider rested his palm on Sandler's back, opened their bedroom door, and guided him into the room first. Before Rider went in, he glanced at Drew and said, "Are you sure you don't mind me sleeping with Sandler? I mean, *we're* definitely not a couple anymore, right?"

Drew shrugged. "Of course we're not a couple. I don't care where you sleep."

"I was just wondering, especially after what happened the other night at your place in West Hollywood." Whenever Drew used that superior tone, he wasn't playing around.

"I told you that was strictly sex and you're free to do whatever you want, Rider. And I couldn't care less what you do or with whom you do it," Drew said. "Now if you'll excuse me, I'm going to unpack and take a nap. I'm exhausted. I'll see you at dinner."

"Okay," Rider said. "I just wanted to be certain. Have a nice nap." Then he went into his room to join Sandler without giving Drew a chance to reply.

CHAPTER SIX

A few minutes before dinner that night, Rider, Sandler, and Drew met downstairs in the main hall. Drew and Sandler had been waiting there for twenty minutes, and Rider didn't find this odd in the least. In fact, it was a novelty for Rider to be on time. He usually showed up twenty minutes late wherever he went. It's not that he didn't try to be on time. He couldn't help it if his hair didn't go the right way, or his sideburns needed a little extra trim. And of course there were those times when he looked in the mirror and realized his outfit was all wrong...or it made his butt look fat...and he had to change clothes all over again at the last minute.

When Drew saw Rider coming down the stairs, he smiled and said, "Well, look at that. You're right on time instead of twenty minutes

76

late as usual." He turned to Sandler and said, "We're lucky. I've waited hours for him just to get his eyebrows right."

Sandler nodded with an awkward gesture that suggested he was scratching the top of his head.

Rider returned Drew's smile and said, "I didn't know you were keeping track of my comings and goings, Drew. Thanks for your support and concern." Rider knew from that tone Drew was trying to say, "Fuck you," in code. But he didn't want to give Drew the satisfaction of replying with more sarcasm, so he simply smiled and said, "You're looking well tonight, Drew." He did look good, even better than usual. He was wearing a casual gray sport jacket with a tight fit, and light beige slim-fit pants that hugged his legs in all the right places.

"Thanks for *your* support," Drew said. Then he turned at the bottom of the stairs and headed into the dining room without returning the compliment.

Although Jade had mentioned to them that dinner would be what they considered country casual in Vermont, Rider wasn't sure exactly what that meant. He decided to wear one of his more casual skinny suits in a light shade of olive, with a white shirt, and he'd loaned Sandler a dark gray plaid sport jacket to wear with a pair of faded jeans and a white shirt.

When Rider noticed Sandler hadn't packed anything but jeans and pull over shirts, he figured he'd better loan him something a little more formal. Rider had a feeling that the term "country casual" with these pretentious gay guys could mean anything from a white dinner jacket to a simple black dress with a circle pin.

"Do I look okay?" Sandler asked.

Rider reached up and adjusted the collar on his white shirt. "You look great. You're the cutest boy here. Let's go and join them." Then he set his palm on the small of Sandler's back and led him into the dining room without even thinking twice about it. He had to admit the way Sandler seemed to depend on him for guidance excited him. No one had ever looked up to him that way before. Although he knew Sandler was brilliant at what he did professionally, there was also something backward and innocent about the way he handled himself socially. He'd also watched Sandler getting dressed in the room they were sharing. He'd only seen him in his white boxer shorts, but from what he'd seen the guy had long solid legs covered with the perfect amount of black hair, a lean solid torso, and hands the size of dinner plates. All this combined with his messy, dark wavy hair and crystal blue eyes sent Rider's imagination into its highest gear. He'd made a point not to stare at him for too long while they'd been dressing, but Rider couldn't deny he had noticed something long and thick swinging between his legs beneath the white cotton boxer shorts.

They found Thorn, Jade, Drew and a few other people they didn't know already seated at the table. It wasn't as a large a group as Rider had expected. When Thorn saw them, he gestured toward two vacant chairs and said, "Welcome. Rider, you can sit next to my Aunt Betty, and Sandler, you can sit across from Rider, beside Drew."

When Sandler hesitated for a moment, Drew said, "Don't worry Sandler, nothing will happen to you if you're separated from Rider during dinner. Come sit next to me."

Sandler looked at Rider, in the most adorable way, as if to ask for permission and Rider said, "It's okay. Go on."

In order to explain the look Sandler had given him, Rider laughed and spoke to them all. "He looks up to me like a big brother or something."

"You definitely are something," Drew said, with that same deadpan tone he always used whenever he was angry about something.

"And you are something *else*, Drew," Rider said.

Drew smiled and smoothed out his napkin. "Thank you."

"Don't mention it," Rider said.

After that, there was a moment of awkward silence, and then Thorn introduced everyone to the other people sitting around the table. Two of them worked in production for the film company Jade and Thorn owned. Their names were Jackson and Kendall, and then there was Aunt Betty from Boston. Jackson looked as if he preferred pizza and doughnuts to salad and fruit. He wore a bright red sweater that pulled across his stomach and a camel sport jacket he couldn't button. Kendall was one of those fair-skinned natural blonds, with a Roman nose, a weak chin, and thin lips. He was wearing a denim jacket with a black mock turtleneck and Rider was beginning to feel a bit overdressed. At least Aunt Betty had taken the time to put on a simple black and gray dress. Her hair was platinum and a little too puffy. It looked as if she'd been wearing it the same way since the 1970s. She seemed harmless enough, though. She was sitting there holding a black purse on her lap as if she was worried someone might snatch it.

No one actually got up and shook hands. They simply nodded and smiled. The dining room table was one of those long modern affairs, with some kind of abstract wooden base and a narrow glass top. Noting about it fit in with the renovated barn look, which didn't surprise Rider.

Jade and Thorn seemed to be making that statement everywhere he looked. The only issue was that Rider couldn't figure out what their statement was.

The dinner conversation consisted mainly of Thorn talking about all of his accomplishments and achievements while Jade nodded and backed him up. They weren't exactly the kind of accomplishments anyone would consider leaning forward to hear, and he used the word "mundane" so often it became ironic. Aside from the fact that he'd won a few industry awards for the porn films he'd produced, Rider came to the conclusion that the most interesting thing that had happened to Thorn in the last forty years was that he'd now owned a Bentley.

As a couple, Jade and Thorn had an interesting arrangement. Thorn sat there telling long stories about himself while Jade finished preparing the dinner, serving the dinner, and cleaning up after everyone had finished dinner. But more than that, Jade didn't seem to mind in the least. If anything he tended to get up from the table to do something every time Thorn started one of his long stories, and he smiled all the way into the kitchen.

Kendall and Jackson behaved as typical employees would behave during dinner with their boss. They laughed at Jade's quips, nodded in agreement with his comments, and shrugged when he didn't agree with something. They reminded Rider of the kind of kowtowing guys who would even switch their deepest political convictions if their boss suggested it. Drew said very little during dinner, which didn't surprise Rider. Drew tended to evaluate and assess people and situations without letting them know it. He had this fascinating way of looking at people while they talked, as if they were the only person in the room...or on the planet for that matter. And while Drew did this he was usually plotting his strategies in order to be a few steps ahead of them.

Although it wasn't too obvious, Drew and Rider continued to throw shade at each from across the table. And they stopped conversation several times, especially when Rider smiled and said, "Drew's most endearing charm in life is his ability to break people down over long periods of time."

Drew sent Rider a bigger smile from across the table and said, "And Rider's most endearing charm is his ability to *pretend* he's letting people break them down over long periods of time so he can get all the control."

The only one who offered the slightest hint of light amusement was Aunt Betty, and even then it was through no fault of her own. She sat there smiling and nodding at all of Thorn's stories, with total adoration. When Thorn stopped talking…which didn't happen often…she would send Jade a look and give him a little dig. She didn't do this in an obnoxious way. Jade had prepared a pulled pork main course that night, which Rider thought was actually very good. Aunt Betty seemed to think otherwise. She didn't come out and say she didn't like it, but she did say, "I love the cuisines of the lower classes, Jade. How wonderful that you're so good at preparing them. It's a gift to be so ordinary."

Nothing Jade did seemed to please Aunt Betty, and she let everyone know this with smiles and light-hearted comments that had to be parsed to get the full under-lying meaning. Rider nearly fell over sideways at the beginning of the meal when she lifted her fork and said, "Jade, dear, I have smudges on my fork and I don't think it's been washed properly. I do hate to be a bother, but I'm not used to using inexpensive unwashed flatware." Rider had to give her credit for that one. It was a double zinger and she didn't even seem to be trying too hard. She'd not only insulted Jade's housekeeping, but it was obvious they were using real silverware that night, not cheap flatware.

After dinner, they all went into what Thorn referred to as the "keeping room," for an after dinner drink, and to talk about the wedding. When they entered, Rider noticed that the entire room had been decorated for Christmas. There wasn't a fall pumpkin or gourd to be seen, as if they'd hopped right over Halloween and Thanksgiving that year and plunged right into the holiday season. He poked Drew in the arm with his elbow and said, "They're a little early with the Christmas decorations, don't you think?"

Drew smiled and spoke softly. "Didn't I tell you? This is going to be a Christmas wedding? It's a theme wedding. Thorn has always wanted to be married at Christmastime, so they decorated this room for the holidays. The feature we're doing for the web site won't be out until December, so it works."

"No. You didn't tell me. You're joking?" Rider asked. He glanced around the room again. It was another version of odd mid-century modern mixed with Shaker primitive pieces, but as minimalist as possible. The only difference was that room had a massive white Christmas tree with multicolored lights, orange and purple ornaments, and kitschy holiday paraphernalia draped everywhere he looked. There were so many drugstore fake Santa Clauses he worked hard to keep his expression blank. But more than that, if something wasn't covered with glitter, it was sprayed in gold.

"Of course not," Drew said. "I think it's a wonderful angle. Our readers will love it. Who doesn't love Christmastime, especially when it's gay?"

Rider sighed and said, "Bah humbug. This room looks as if Santa's sleigh crashed into it." He'd never been a fan of exploiting anything "gay" for the sake of getting attention, and yet he knew that was part of what they were doing with the web site and he couldn't complain.

Drew smiled, as if they were having a cheerful conversation. "It's not that bad. Just shut up, pretend it's Christmas, and spread some god damn good holiday cheer."

Rider just frowned and crossed to a hard mid-century modern sofa and kidney shaped coffee table and sat down next to Sandler. When he sat down on it, it felt like a park bench. For the next few hours, he watched Aunt Betty…who claimed she didn't drink much…polish off a bottle of Port and he listened to Thorn tell a story about each Christmas decoration in the room. The ornaments on the tree came from Poland, the plastic garland that draped the white marble fireplace had been custom designed in Montana, and the electric train set around the base of the Christmas tree was one of the rarest vintage finds he'd ever made. Everything had a story, and Aunt Betty wanted to hear the stories repeated twice. The only one who didn't have to sit through all this was Jade. He kept coming and going from the kitchen, claiming he wanted to get everything cleaned up so that there wouldn't be a mess in the morning. Rider was tempted to offer his help. He would have mopped the kitchen floor to get out of all those long stories.

By the time Rider glanced at his watch and saw it was almost midnight, he started to get that panicky feeling that this nightmare would never end. He would wind up trapped there, in this unusual room, surrounded by surreal Christmas decorations, while Thorn told stories about himself until the end of days. He was doomed and there was no way out.

Thanks to Aunt Betty, Thorn finally stopped talking. He was right in the middle of that time when he was on a cruise in the South Pacific and the most interesting thing happened to him when Aunt Betty nodded off and started snoring. He tried to continue talking through the snores, as if she wasn't even in the room, but she let out one huge snort, followed by a gag, and everyone turned to see if she was still alive.

Thorn called Jade into the keeping room and said, "I think you should get Aunt Betty upstairs now."

Rider wondered why Thorn didn't get her up to bed. She was *his* aunt.

Jade glanced at her and smiled. "She sure did knock them down tonight. I think she broke her own record for Port."

That's when Rider stood up and stretched his arms. "It's been a delightful evening, Thorn, and I love listening to you talk about yourself, but I'm exhausted myself. I think I'll be going upstairs, too." He smiled at Jade. He was starting to feel sorry for him. "And dinner was fantastic. Thank you."

Drew sent Rider a dirty look, as if he'd said something wrong.

Sandler stood up fast and said, "Yes. I'll come with you. I'm feeling tired, too."

Aunt Betty snorted again and mumbled some kind of gibberish in her sleep.

Then the two employees, Kendall and Jackson, stood up and said they were ready to head out to the studio where they were sleeping that night. As far as Rider could tell, they weren't part of the feature story or the wedding. They were headed back to their respective homes the following morning and they'd only been invited to dinner as a gesture from Jade and Thorn.

"I suppose it is getting late," Thorn said. "I'll see you all in the morning. Right now I have to help Jade get Aunt Betty upstairs safely. We don't want any broken hips this weekend."

Then Drew stood up and he thanked Jade and Thorn for a nice evening. He followed Rider and Sandler upstairs and turned to the left when they reached their rooms.

"Have a good night's sleep, Drew," Rider said.

"Thank you," Drew said. "You sleep well, too." He smiled at Sandler. "I'll see you both in the morning and we can talk about the feature a little more. I'd like Sandler to start getting photos tomorrow. Remember, we're still working while we're here. This isn't a vacation."

Rider and Sandler waited for Drew to go into his room, and then Rider opened their door and gestured for Sandler to go inside first. The moment they were inside and the door was closed, Rider fell back on the bed and said, "I never thought that night would end. They're nice guys, and I really like Jade, but when Thorn tells a story he never wants to land that proverbial plane."

Sandler laughed in a quiet way. "I have to admit he does tell long stories."

"Dear God," Rider said. "That guy should have been a priest or a politician. I've never met anyone who can talk about nothing at all for so long."

Sandler laughed into his hand in a shy way. "And that story he told about how he bought this property in Vermont we're in right now. Is it me? There wasn't anything unusual about it. It was just a story about buying property with nothing special."

"Ha-ha. And it lasted for an hour."

Sandler laughed and walked over to a chair where he'd left his suitcase. As he removed the jacket Rider had loaned him and placed it neatly over the back of a chair, Rider noticed how nicely the jeans hugged his small buttocks. Everything about him was sexy in a quiet way. He wasn't a muscle jock, but he had a firm body. His dark wavy hair wasn't too short like most of the gay guys Rider knew, but it wasn't too long either. He could have been described as either a hipster or an average guy in college, but he wasn't really either one. He didn't actually cross any particular lines. He seemed to fall in between them.

While Sandler was getting undressed, Rider stood up and crossed to a small loveseat near the fireplace where he'd left his suitcase. "I hope you don't mind that I sleep in the nude," he said. "I can't stand sleeping in clothes." He said this because he wanted to get a reaction.

"I don't mind," Sandler said. "I sleep naked, too. I hope *you* don't mind."

"Not at all," Rider said. "In fact, I think this is going to work out even better than I thought it would."

CHAPTER SEVEN

On weekends when there was nothing to do, Rider liked to watch cooking shows on PBS. Even though he didn't cook often, he told himself that he would start cooking eventually, when he had more time. One of those TV shows had a young junior chef on once in a while. The guy had thick dark hair, a slim body, dark scruff all over his face, and he wore glasses that always seemed too large for his face. He wasn't someone that would have stood out in a crowd for most people, but something about him...his overall look...made Rider want to rip off his own clothes and bend over furniture.

Sandler reminded Rider of this guy on the cooking show on TV, and that night in the bedroom they were sharing in Vermont he wanted to see if he could fulfill another one of his sexual fantasies. Even though he still had strong feelings for Drew, he wasn't with Drew at that moment, and he wasn't planning on being with Drew any time soon. For all he knew, he and Drew would never be a couple again. And even though he would have preferred sleeping with Drew that night, he wasn't going to ignore the fact that he was, indeed, sleeping with Sandler.

While Rider removed all of his clothes and rested them on the loveseat, Sandler did the same on the other side of the room and he set his clothes on the chair. Rider had never been ashamed of his body and he didn't mind getting naked in front of anyone. He worked out several times a week and he did have distinct muscle definition. Although he wasn't huge like some of the weight lifters he saw, and he didn't have those creepy looking abs that some weight lifters strive for, he knew his body could compete with the best of the models he saw in magazines. And while his body had never been a top priority in his life, he did know how to use it to his advantage whenever necessary.

On that particular night in the room he was sharing with Sandler, he crossed naked to the other side where Sandler was still undressing so he could get the TV remote he'd noticed on a table near the window earlier that day. When he passed by Sandler, acting as if being naked in front of him was perfectly normal, he noticed Sandler had a hairy chest and abdomen that complimented the hair on his legs. He still hadn't removed his boxer shorts yet. Rider walked around him, gently touched his arm, and said, "Excuse me, cutie. I just want to get the TV remote."

The instant Rider called him cutie Sandler's cheeks turned red and he fumbled for a response. He tried not to look at Rider's naked body but his eyes did a few quick downward turns. "Um, ok. I'll move."

Rider rubbed his arm gently and said, "You're fine. You're not in the way. There's plenty of room for both of us." Then he slid past him and slowly walked over to get the TV remote. He took his time on purpose. He even leaned over a little to pick the remote up because he knew Sandler was staring at his ass. Although Sandler didn't know this, Rider could see Sandler's reflection in a mirror on the wall above the headboard, and he was definitely watching every move Rider made.

While Sandler removed his boxer shorts, Rider turned off the light on the nightstand next to his bed and climbed on top of the bed. Even though the room was darker, he could still see everything Sandler was doing. And when he noticed what was swinging back and forth between Sandler's legs after he removed his boxers, he blinked and leaned forward slightly. Rider had never been one of those people who cared about the size of a man's penis. He was slightly above average himself and he'd never been self-conscious about his own penis. He'd

Ryan Field

once dated a guy who a penis so small it reminded him of his own pinky

finger…erect…and he'd still had good sex with the guy and his penis size

made no difference to Rider whatsoever. He'd been with men of all kinds

and their penis size had never been a priority. The only thing Rider had

never seen so far was a flaccid penis so long and thick it reminded him of

a ring bologna. He tried not to stare at Sandler's dick for too long, but he

couldn't help wondering how big it got when it was erect.

"I'm going to brush my teeth," Sandler said. He headed toward

the small on suite bathroom.

"I'll try to find something on TV," Rider said. He was on the bed,

in the middle, on all fours with his legs spread. He was about to pull back

the covers, but he wanted Sandler to see him in this position before he

did that. If they were going to do anything that night he wanted Sandler

to be the one to initiate it. Sandler was a few years younger and he

seemed so innocent. Rider didn't like feeling as if he was preying on

someone so good and decent. Even though that's what he was thinking,

he decided to play it cool and let Sandler make the first move. And if he

didn't, Rider could live with that, too.

While Sandler was in the bathroom brushing his teeth, Rider

pulled a few condoms and some lube out of his suitcase and placed them in the nightstand drawer just in case. Then he pulled the covers back and repositioned the pillows. The bedding was simple white cotton, and he suspected it was the highest thread count made. It felt silky and he had a feeling Thorn and Jade never settled for anything less than the very best. The white duvet trimmed with black piping smelled as if they'd used mountain fresh scent detergent. It was one of those high queen size beds, with a thick quilt top mattress. Rider noticed they'd added a few extra layers of foam rubber to make the bed even taller and more cushioned. With each move he made he sank in a little deeper. Even though he preferred his lower, firmer platform bed in California, it was a nice change and he was looking forward to Sandler...and his hairy legs...joining him in this soft, fluffy bed.

When Sandler emerged from the bathroom, he crossed toward the bed with his dick swinging back and forth in the most obnoxious, and yet innocent, way. He wasn't doing it on purpose, which was obvious; he couldn't help it. It seemed to move around as if it had a life of its own and Rider wanted to grab it and examine it more closely.

Rider had already rested back on the side of the bed closest to the wall so Sandler wouldn't have to climb over him. A mistake and it was already too late to rectify that. He should have taken the other side so

Rider and his big dick had to climb over him. He would have enjoyed watching it swing back and forth over his face.

"I can't find anything but news channels from Canada," Rider said. "But it's interesting. They have such nice, friendly news up here. I'm used to watching news about murder and crime. So far all I've seen is that there's a moose on the loose somewhere, and they opened a new chocolate shop in some town I never heard of."

Sandler climbed up on the bed and turned to rest back against the pillows. "I've never been this far up north in the US. It's all unfamiliar to me." He smelled as if he'd put on some kind of cologne, and he'd combed his hair a little. Rider wondered if he'd sink washed his junk as well.

"I haven't either," Rider said. "I guess we're both virgins in that respect." Then he laughed to let him know he was only joking around.

Sandler took a quick breath and asked, "Do you mind if I turn out the light?"

The only light in the room other than the TV came from the lamp on the nightstand next to him. It wasn't very bright. "No, not at all. It's been a long day and I'm kind of tired."

He turned off the light and said, "Oh. I see."

"I'm not *that* tired," Rider said. "Do you mind if I watch a little TV for a while?"

"No," Sandler said. "I'm not that tired either. Put on anything you want. I'll watch with you."

While Sandler pulled the duvet up to his chest and adjusted his position, Rider switched through all the channels until he finally found a movie that looked interesting. It was something he'd seen a long time ago, a horror film that had no redeeming qualities other than hot young guys who drink too much, and clueless young women who always go down to the dark creepy basement alone.

"I hope you don't mind a horror film," Rider said. "I can't find anything else and this one isn't half bad. I saw it a long time ago."

"I like horror films," Sandler said. "This is fine."

For the next 20 minutes, they watched the film in silence. The only light in the room came from the TV, which was enough to make out the outline of Sandler's long hairy legs beneath the duvet. Sandler hardly moved at all, and when he did Rider kept getting a whiff of whatever cologne he'd used. It was something spicy and deep and it reminded him of a cologne Boris used to wear.

When it became apparent Sandler wasn't going to make the first move, Rider decided it was time to try a different strategy. At one point in the film, during a scene that had been designed to make people scream, Rider jumped and reached over to grab Sandler's arm.

"I'm sorry," Rider said with his most innocent tone. "I don't normally jump like that, but that scene took me by surprise. I don't think I'd watch this scary movie if you weren't here with me."

Sandler laughed, and then he put his arm about Rider. "I think it's cute. Come over here and I'll protect you."

Without making it too obvious, Rider moved up against Sandler's side and rested his palm on his chest.

Sandler put his arm around him tighter and asked, "Is that better?"

Rider rubbed his hairy chest and said, "Much better, cutie."

They continued watching the movie for a few more minutes, and then Rider threw his leg over Sandler's and said, "This bed is so comfortable, and you smell so good. I like it."

"Thanks," Sandler said. "It's nothing special. Just some body spray from the drugstore."

"I like it a lot," Rider said. He figured that Sandler had already made the first move when he'd put his arm around him and pulled him closer. It seemed as if that was the most logical conclusion. It was up to him to make the next move, and he knew it. So he slowly ran his hand down Sandler's body and rested it on his dick. His dick was pointed to the right and he was already fully erect. Rider couldn't even get his entire hand around it. His heart started beating faster and he had to tell himself to remain calm. "This feels nice, too."

Sandler spread his legs a little so Rider could get a better grip. "Is this okay? What we're doing. We work together and you're my boss." He stammered a little when he said boss.

Rider brought his dick up so that it could rest on his lower abdomen. He stroked it gently and said, "Technically, I'm not your boss. Boris is *our* boss. We all work for him. I'm just the writer and I have creative input. So, technically, we're just working together."

"So what we're doing right now is okay?"

Rider found this conversation a little tedious. All he wanted to do was get his entire hand around his dick. "Do you want to stop?"

"No."

"Neither do I."

"Just one more thing," Sandler said.

"What?"

"Do you mind that I'm so big?" Sandler asked.

"I don't understand," Rider said. It was the last thing he expected to hear.

"My penis is unusually large," Sandler said. "Does that bother you?"

"Not in the least," Rider said. "I would never mention anyone's penis size."

The next thing Rider knew he was flat on his back and Sandler was on top of him. Without warning, Sandler turned into this dominant, aggressive lover that left Rider speechless. Sandler kicked the covers right off the bed and forced Rider to the middle. Rider grabbed his shoulders and he spread Rider's legs apart. When Sandler climbed on top of him, Rider lifted his legs and they kissed so intensely Rider couldn't hear the TV anymore. While Sandler's huge dick pressed into his lower abdomen, Rider ran his hands up and down his strong back as if to draw him in closer. It wasn't possible for them to get any closer, but Rider wanted him so much at that moment he didn't stop trying.

When it became obvious that Sandler would make all the aggressive moves that night, Rider submitted and followed his every gesture. When they stopped kissing and Sandler climbed up and sat on his chest, Rider opened his mouth and started sucking as much of his dick as he could. It was impossible to get more than a third of it into his mouth, and he'd sucked some big cocks in his time. He tried as hard as he could. While Sandler rested back on his legs, with his dick in Rider's mouth, he closed his eyes and let Rider do all the work. He moaned a little, and even grunted a few times. He seemed to like what Rider was doing, so Rider continued until Sandler decided it was time to change positions again.

When he finally pulled his dick out of Rider's mouth, he grabbed Rider by the waist, turned him over, and forced him forward until he was face down on the mattress. Rider said, "You're very strong for such a gentle, polite man."

"Is it too rough?" Sandler asked. There was a hint of panic in his voice.

"No. I know I can trust you," Rider said. "You obviously know what you're doing."

Then Sandler climbed on top of him and shoved his dick up against his ass. When he started moving his hips and rubbing his dick up and down Rider's ass, he said, "You're so smooth."

Rider spread his legs a little wider and said, "I have condoms and lube. I put them in the nightstand drawer."

"You did?" He laughed. "I have them, too. I put them in my nightstand drawer when you weren't looking."

There was no point in denying they'd obviously been thinking along the same lines. "Let's use yours," Rider said. "They're probably larger than mine." The condoms he'd brought along were pretty generic...he'd picked them up for free at his dentist's office...and he was hoping Sandler had the extra-large size he often saw as his local Rite Aid but never bothered to purchase.

While Sandler put on the condom, Rider got up and reached for the lube. He wanted to spread some around himself before they started, to make sure he didn't miss anything. He was far from a virgin, but he spread his legs extra wide, squeezed a generous amount of lube on his fingers, and reached around to get it everywhere.

After Sandler lubed the condom covering his dick, he asked, "How should we do this?"

He'd been so aggressive up until that point Rider had expected him to just take control and fuck him from behind, which is what most aggressive men usually did. Rider was grateful this one time, and he smiled and said, "I think you should get on your back and I should straddle you. I think it'll be easier that way."

"Are you sure?" Sandler asked. "We don't have to do this. There are other things we can do."

"I'm sure," Rider said. Oh, he had to do this.

As Sandler rested on his back in the middle of the bed, Rider threw his leg over Sandler's waist and positioned his bottom right above Sandler's erection. He arched his back and Sandler grabbed him by the waist. He reached back and grabbed Sandler's. It took a minute or two to get the head inside; he had to work it in slowly and relax his sphincter completely.

Sandler held his waist tighter and asked, "Is it too big?"

It felt as if a baseball bat had entered his body and he wasn't sure he could get beyond the pain. However, he nodded and said, "I'm good," and then he slowly lowered his bottom to see if he could take more of him.

At first, he felt the pain all the way up to his temples, and it wasn't even halfway in. But he continued, with ease, to take him completely. By the time most of it was inside him, he rested his palms on Sandler's stomach, arched his back and little more, and took a deep breath.

"Are you okay?" Sandler asked.

He exhaled and said, "I'm good." He'd already passed the initial pain and his body had relaxed. "I just want to sit here like this for a minute or two until I'm ready to move again. I want to get used to you." He was trying to control his breathing; he'd already broken a sweat.

Sandler removed one hand from his waist and slapped his ass. "You can sit there like this as long as you want. I don't mind in the least."

Rider smiled. "I'll bet you don't."

Although the size of him still felt foreign, and even a little dangerous, he eventually started grinding his hips slowly. Sandler moaned and rubbed his hips. "That's feels nice," he said. "No one's ever done that."

"No one?" Rider found that hard to believe.

Sandler shook his head. "I'm not that experienced."

"Are you a virgin?"

"Kind of. But not totally."

"What does that mean?" He was still grinding slowly and he didn't want to stop. The pain had stopped and he never felt anything quite like this before. And even though he hated to admit it, he was beginning to wonder if size really did matter.

"I've been with guys, I've had sex with them, but I've never actually fucked anyone before," he said. "It's always been kind of casual sex, you know, but never anal."

Rider understood this, as most gay men would. Having sex with a man didn't always lead to anal sex. In fact, the most casual sex rarely did lead to anal sex. "I'm glad I'm the first."

Then Rider started riding his dick a little faster. Sandler grabbed him by the waist and he started moving his hips. They found a rhythm that made things more intense. They never spoke a word, but Rider couldn't keep from moaning aloud. That huge dick was stimulating parts of Rider's body he didn't even know existed. It reached a point where it sounded more like screaming. Sandler tried stuffing Rider's mouth with his large fingers, but even that didn't stop Rider from making the most obnoxious noses. The headboard started knocking into the wall, and they

Ryan Field

continued until the bed rocked and moved away from the wall. Rider didn't care if anyone heard them; very little mattered at that point.

Although neither of them kept track of time, later Rider would come to the conclusion they'd fucked in this position for at least a half hour without stopping. He would know this later that night, because the movie they'd been watching would end, and he would also know this because he would be a little sore the following morning when he sat down for breakfast. However, at that moment, the only thing they cared about was reaching climax. And when they both did reach it, and they both let out loud sounds of exasperation at the same time, Rider wondered if he would ever be the same man again after experiencing a dick like that.

Of course that was an exaggeration...maybe even sarcasm in the mind of a man who loved his sex...because when he finally opened his eyes and glanced down at Sandler he smiled and said, "Dude, I think I forgot my name."

Sandler slapped his ass and said, "That was good, man. Let's do it again in the morning. I'll make you forget what year it is next time."

106

"I only regret one thing," Rider said. "I wish I could see what we look like. To be honest, I didn't think I could take a man as big as you are. I'd like to see what it looks like inside me."

Sandler laughed. He reached over to the night stand for his phone and said, "No problem." Then he started taking photos of them in this position. He even reached around and took a photo of his dick buried in Rider's ass, which Rider found highly entertaining.

A few minutes later Sandler pulled out and Rider rolled over rested on his back. He looked at the photos on Sandler's phone and smiled. "I know it looks painful, but that's not how it felt."

Sandler turned off the TV and the room went almost completely dark. He pushed the bed back to where it had been, with the headboard against the wall.

There was moonlight filtering in through the windows now and Rider felt a wave of exhaustion take over. When Sandler climbed back into bed, Rider put the phone on the nightstand and yawned, making a mental note to never let Drew see those photos of him getting fucked. That's all Drew needed to see. There weren't any headshots and no one could identify them, but Drew would know.

Then Rider stretched and yawned again. He hadn't stopped running around since they'd left the West Coast earlier that morning and he found it difficult to keep his eyes open. He moved up against Sandler's warm body and rested his head on his chest. "Good night," he said. "I think you wore me out."

Sandler put his arms around Rider and ran his hand all the way down his back. "I hope no one heard us. I'll die of embarrassment. What we just did...that's not like me. I've never been with anyone who made the furniture move."

Rider sighed and said, "I can think of worse ways to die than embarrassment. Besides, I'm the one who was screaming." He lifted one leg and threw it over Sandler's legs. Sandler was rubbing his bottom and all he wanted to do was close his eyes and sleep.

CHAPTER EIGHT

"Well, well," Drew said. He looked up from the tablet at which he'd been staring. "I see you're having a little trouble walking this morning, Rider. Is it your back?"

Rider had just walked into the dining room where Jade had set up a light buffet with the standard bed and breakfast fare. "Good morning, Drew. I guess my back is acting up a little. It must be from sleeping on a strange mattress." He glanced at the fresh fruit and homemade muffins and made a face. All he wanted was strong black coffee. He'd never been a muffin fan. The word muffin alone made him gag.

"Or maybe it's because you *were* the mattress," Drew said. He was sitting at the long glass table, sipping coffee, staring at his tablet, and eating a small dish of strawberries. He was wearing one of his typical

Drew outfits: a crisp white dress shirt, tight jeans, and loafers without socks.

"Now what's *that* supposed to mean?" Rider said, as he limped to the table trying to keep the coffee from splashing out of his mug. He probably shouldn't have let Sandler fuck him again that morning. From the waist down, everything was sore.

Drew smiled. He sat back and took another sip of coffee. "Oh please," he said. "It's not as if you were discreet. From the moans and bangs and screams I heard last night, and this morning, from the way you two were going at, it I'm surprised you can even get out of bed. I just hope you left poor Sandler in one piece."

Rider was in no mood to bicker or exchange insults that morning. "I have no idea what you're talking about. You must have been dreaming. And even if I did know what you were talking about, it's really none of your business because we're not a couple anymore and you have no control over what I do, or with whom I do it."

"Well, that's always been clear," Drew said. "Even when we were a couple I never had any control over what you did, or with whom you did it."

"I'd rather not get into that again," Rider said. "I've already explained myself and I've apologized. What more do you want? Would you like a pint of my blood?"

Drew laughed, as if he couldn't have cared less. "That won't be necessary. I've forgiven you. Besides, I know you just can't help yourself. You'll never be happy with just one man."

"That's *not* true."

"Isn't it?" Drew asked.

Then Sandler walked into the dining room and pounded his chest as if he were about to mimic Tarzan. He smiled, walked to the buffet with a spring in his step, and said, "This looks wonderful. I'm starved this morning. I could eat everything here."

"Help yourself," Drew said. "I'm sure you are starved."

Sandler turned and tilted his head sideways. "Huh?"

Rider sent Drew a glance.

"I only mean it must be this Vermont country air," Drew said. "It does give one a good appetite."

"Oh," Sandler said, turning toward the buffet. He looked at the food as if he wanted to jump on top of the buffet table and have sex with it.

"Be good," Rider said to Drew. He didn't want to make Sandler feel uncomfortable.

"I didn't do anything," said Drew. "He's a growing boy. Isn't that right, Sandler? He needs his nutrition to keep up his stamina."

Rider didn't want to drag Sandler into their personal issues. It wasn't fair. The poor guy was only an innocent bystander and Drew had no right to make him feel awkward.

Sandler was staring at the muffins, deciding whether to take a blueberry or bran.

Drew took another sip of coffee and asked Rider, "Have you started working on your story yet? Have you had a chance to interview anyone?"

"You know damn well I haven't," Rider said. "I just got here yesterday. But don't worry. I'll get on that today. I've never missed a deadline in my life and I don't intend to now."

"That's true," Drew said. "In that single respect, I know I can trust you. You've always had superior work ethics."

Sandler sat down on the other side of the table with a huge plate of food that looked as if he'd sampled everything on the buffet twice. He seemed to be paying more attention to the blueberry muffins than Rider and Drew.

"Stop doing that," Rider said to Drew.

"What?"

"You know," Rider said. "Stop making me feel guilty."

Drew stood up and said, "I can assure you that I have no idea what you're talking about, Rider. If you feel guilty it has nothing to do with me." He looked at the way Sandler was gulping down the muffin and smiled. "If you'll excuse me, I'm going upstairs to get a few notes together and send a few e-mails to the office. It's too early for anyone to be there, but I want them to be kept up to date on what's going on while we're here. I want this feature to run smoothly."

As Drew walked out of the dining room, Rider took a huge gulp of coffee and sat back in his chair. He wondered why Drew always had to be that way. He always came off as so superior to everyone else. Even the way he spoke was filled with so much condescension Rider often felt like shoving a butt plug up his ass while he was in the middle of the most common sentence. But even more than that, Rider wondered why he'd always found Drew's condescension so attractive. Even then, on that morning, long after they'd been a couple, he still felt something for Drew he found hard to explain that transcended the sex he'd had with Sandler.

By the time he finished his coffee and was ready for another, he glanced across the table and saw Sandler ready to get up and head back to the buffet table. He'd finished his entire plate of food without saying a word.

"Can I get you anything?" Sandler asked.

Rider nodded. "More coffee, please. Black."

Sandler winked at him and turned. "Are you sure you don't want any food? You might want to keep up your strength for what's coming later."

"I'm good," Rider said. He smiled but he wasn't sure how to react. Now that Sandler knew he *could* fuck him, that seemed to be the only thing on his mind. Rider understood that it was only natural for him to feel this way. The poor guy had never actually fucked anyone before, and he hated to turn him down. They'd fucked in bed very early that morning and then again in the shower less than two hours later.

The guy had one thing on his mind and Rider wasn't sure if he could continue saying yes. It wasn't that Rider was worried about any emotional attachments. They'd discussed that already and both made it clear this was nothing more than sex. In fact, Sandler was the one who brought the topic up in the first place, just to be sure that Rider didn't get the wrong idea. That's how they wound up fucking again in the shower. When Rider agreed that he wasn't interested in anything more than just sex, Sandler slapped him on the ass and practically pulled him into the shower stall. It was amazing to watch how aggressive he could be in this kind of a situation. He didn't even ask for permission that time. After he turned on the shower, he turned Rider around so that he was facing the subway tiles on the wall, put on a condom, and entered him with a loud sigh. Rider just spread his legs and braced his palms on the tiles. It took less than ten minutes and Rider didn't even come that time. For the first time in Rider's life he felt like a human blow up doll, which was oddly satisfying and slightly confusing.

After Rider finished his second cup of coffee, they both rose from the table at the same time and Sandler headed back to their room so he could connect with the office and work on a few tech issues for the upcoming launch. Although Rider understood enough about technology to do what he had to do as a writer and editor, he didn't know even a fraction of the details that went into launching a new web site and the best he could do was pretend he understood so he wouldn't appear to be a blithering idiot.

As he left the room, Sandler winked at Rider again and said, "If you'd like to join me up there I wouldn't mind. You could take off your pants and sit on my lap."

Rider had a feeling all the food Sandler had eaten for breakfast had energized him and Rider didn't feel like getting fucked that soon again. Even the backs of his legs were sore. He needed at least a few hours to get into the mood again. "I'm only going to work," he said. "I have to interview a few people this morning. I'll catch up with you later."

Sandler winked again and sent him a thumb up. "Catch you later, man."

As Rider turned to head toward the kitchen, Jade walked into the dining room with a rolling cart. He headed toward the buffet table and started to clear it without saying a word to Rider. It didn't appear to be a slight. He simply seemed happy about what he was doing.

"Can I give you a hand?" Rider asked.

"Oh, no," Jade said. "I'm used to doing everything around here."

"Where's Thorn, and where is Aunt Betty?" Rider asked. He hadn't seen them come down for breakfast yet and he assumed they wouldn't be down when Jade started clearing the buffet.

Jade laughed while he stacked the cart. "Oh, Thorn never gets up before ten in the morning. He's never been a morning person. And I never speak to him until noon. He can't stand talking in the morning. If I even look at him as if I might say something he starts to cringe."

Rider walked over to the table and started to clear a few of the dishes. He didn't feel comfortable just standing there watching Jade do all the work alone. "I've never been a morning person myself," Rider said. "I'm always amazed at people who can just get up and smile first thing in the morning."

"Thorn can't even stand the sound of a TV before noon," Jade said.

"He sounds very set in his ways," Rider said. Actually, Thorn sounded like a pain in the ass. However, Rider wanted to know more about their relationship for the article he was going to write about them.

Jade laughed even louder that time. "That's putting it mildly. Thorn's a living prick in the morning. But don't repeat that."

Rider smiled. Jade seemed comfortable with him. "I'll never repeat it to anyone." And he wouldn't repeat that to anyone, not even in his article. He'd learned that in order to get to know someone during an interview a certain level of trust had to be obtained. Without that trust, an interview of human interest would always wind up one-dimensional.

After the table and buffet were cleared he followed Jade into the kitchen and said, "I wish you'd let me help. I can stack the dishwasher. The kitchen isn't my favorite room, but I can do that." He glanced around the kitchen and couldn't help commenting on what he saw. "This kitchen isn't like any other room in the house. It's absolutely wonderful. I feel as if I've walked into the eighteenth century." That cabinetry was rustic cherry in a classic shaker style and the ceiling had thick, dark wooden beams. The countertops were all wooden, and there were no cabinets above the counters. Instead, there were shelves stacked neatly with simple beige porcelain and clear glass. The floor had the same wide planks as the rest of the house, but this time they fit perfectly with everything. Rider even noticed the simple, elegant flour sack dish towels. And most of all, there wasn't one of those clichéd center islands that every kitchen in the world seemed to have.

Jade smiled, as if Rider had paid him the most wonderful compliment in the world. "Thank you. I designed it myself. As you can see, I like things simple. And I wanted it to be authentic. This barn was built in the early 1800s. Thorn allowed me to do this one room in the house all alone, and I'm happy with the results. Since I spend most of my time in here, I wanted something I'd always dreamed about, and a place where I could go to get away from everything else. I even have a small work area over in the corner that I use as a small office. I'm not all that fond of the mid-century modern look that Thorn loves so much. It's everywhere in this house, in case you haven't noticed."

"Yes. I did notice," Rider said. "It's nice. Very minimalist." It really made him gag, but he couldn't say that.

"It's just not me," Jade said. "But Thorn loves it, and as long as he's happy I'm happy."

"It sounds as if you make a lot of compromises so Thorn can be happy," Rider said. He was trying to draw more out of Jade without him realizing it.

Jade turned and looked directly at him. "Who doesn't make a lot of compromises in a relationship or marriage? That's what marriage is all about. There's usually one person that's a little stronger than the other, at least on the outside anyway. And there's one who seems to make more compromises than the other. It's a balancing act."

"Would you say that Thorn is the stronger one in your marriage?" Rider asked.

Jade started stacking the dishwasher. It was one of those stainless steel high end affairs with a name that Rider had never been able to pronounce. Jade laughed and said, "Well, I let him think he's the stronger one."

"I don't understand," Rider said.

"How old are you, Rider?"

"I'm 24."

"Oh, you're so young," Jade said. "I'm 42, and thorn is 46. We've been together for over 20 years…forever. When you're with someone for any length of time, you learn how to create a balance that works for you, or for your relationship. It's not always easy either. But once you find that balance, and you see that it works for you, that's something you hold onto. With Thorn and me the balance is that Thorn always thinks he's the one in charge. I let him think that because he has such a huge ego and he's so creative."

Rider tilted his head to the side. "It's like a game?"

"Not exactly," Jade said. "It's more like a dance, a smooth dance where each partner knows how to move without stepping on the other one's foot too many times."

"I'm not sure I understand," Rider said. Evidently, he'd underestimated Jade. He seemed to know exactly what he was doing.

"You will eventually," Jade said. "I see how you're interacting with Drew. You were lovers once, weren't you?"

"For a short time, we were a couple. How did you know that?"

Jade shrugged and closed the dishwasher. "I watched you together."

"It's that obvious?"

"Not really," Jade said. "No one else probably noticed it. I just happen to be good at things like this, is all."

"We're not together anymore," Rider said. "That all ended a couple of years ago. We're only working together now by accident. It wasn't something either of us would have chosen willingly. We both got an offer we couldn't refuse."

"But you could have turned down the offer," Jade said, as he sent him a smile.

"Well, I suppose so."

"You could have turned it down and done something else," Jade said. "No one took you by the arm and forced to both to work together again."

"What are you trying to say?" Rider asked.

"Nothing," Jade said. "I'm just making an observation. I like you both."

Rider laughed. "Who's the one doing the interviewing here?"

Jade walked over to the stove and started arranging food on a large tray. "I'm sorry. I shouldn't have said anything. But I really do like you guys. You actually remind me of the way Thorn and I used to be when we first started out. Drew is a lot like Thorn. He's more serious, less animated, and always needs to be in control."

"There's no reason to apologize," Rider said. "I have to admit that I do get a little crazy whenever I'm in the same room with Drew."

"Then you should be careful," Jade said. "I heard what was going on in your room last night with Sandler."

"Oh, no," Rider said. "I'm so sorry. I hope no one else heard it."

"Everyone heard it," Jade said. "I had to tell Aunt Betty it was big squirrels on the roof so she wouldn't call the police. Poor thing, she thought someone was trying to break the front door down."

"I'm so sorry. I won't let it happen again."

"I don't care, and neither does Thorn. We thought it was amusing," Jade said. "But I'm not so sure that Drew found it amusing. That's all I'm saying."

"Well, I'm afraid that's over with Drew," Rider said. "My relationship with Drew is nothing more than professional now, and it's going to stay that way. So it doesn't matter what Drew thinks."

"If you say so," Jade said. He picked up the tray he'd just loaded with fruit, muffins, coffee, and the small glass of prune juice. "Now I have to take this upstairs to Aunt Betty. You know she *only* eats breakfast in her room."

"Seriously?"

"It's better that way," Jade said. "The last thing you want to see first thing in the morning is *her* face. It's not a pretty sight."

"I gather Aunt Betty is one of the compromises you've made over the years," Rider said.

"Oh yes," he said as he turned toward a back staircase. "Aunt Betty is just one on the invisible list that I've learned to live with, and I know how to handle her. You'll see. It happens to most of us sooner or later. It's not so bad. Trust me, I'm not perfect and Thorn has his own list of compromises with me."

As he watched Jade climb the back staircase, he doubted that. In this particular case he had a feeling Jade made most of the compromises in that relationship, and Thorn got away with whatever he wanted. It seemed to work for them both and Rider wasn't about to judge them, especially when he considered his own relationship with Drew. He also realized this article wasn't going to be as difficult to write as he thought it might be, and it just might save the feature from becoming another piece of awful clickbait about gay couples exploiting themselves and their relationships for the sake of attention.

CHAPTER NINE

After Rider finished speaking with Jade, he went outside to a rear patio that overlooked a long, thin swimming pool to write down a few notes for his article. He wasn't planning to write the actual article there in Vermont. He would do that when he returned to the West Coast, however, he didn't want to leave anything out.

Unlike so many of his peers, Rider still used a small notebook and a pencil for notes like this. It wasn't that he was against technology, and he would eventually produce the finished piece in digital format. He just felt more comfortable working with notes he'd written with his own hand instead of notes he'd recorded on his phone with his thumbs.

According to the local weather report on TV, they were having a warm spell for that time of year. It was sunny and in the mid-fifties that morning. The leaves had turned vibrant shades of red, yellow, gold, and orange and they were just about ready to dangle. Jade and Thorn's property sat atop a hill that overlooked the mountains. There seemed to be a magical view in every direction he glanced. Rider tried to work outside for as long as he could. He wanted to enjoy the beauty that surrounded him. And then each time a breeze came along he pulled his jacket up to his chin and shivered. He was used to Southern California, where anything below 70 degrees required three layers of fleece. To his chagrin, he lasted all of a half hour outside before he went into in the main living room…the one Thorn referred to as the keeping room…where he found a small glass desk near one of the smaller Christmas trees that had been set up for the wedding ceremony.

A few minutes later, Thorn loped into the room wearing tight black skinny jeans and a tight black short sleeve shirt to match. He looked as if he were living in Manhattan instead of Northern Vermont. Even though he was an attractive man in his 40s, the outfit appeared a little too young for him in spite of his well-toned body.

Thorn glanced across the room and saw Rider at the table. "Good morning. I hope you slept well."

Rider smiled. It was half past noon by then. "Very well, thank you. I've never been to this part of the country before and it's absolutely beautiful. I never slept better in my life."

Thorn sent him a look and giggled. "I'll bet. I don't think that bedroom has seen *that* kind of action since that time we shot a scene up there for a gay for pay twink movie we made a few years ago."

Rider shrugged. "It's a very nice bed." He was tired of apologizing and he wasn't going to explain or offer excuses. Didn't these people know how to overlook something like this? That's what he would have done if he'd overheard people having great sex.

Thorn turned and Jade passed through the room carrying a huge stack of thick gray bath towels. Every bathroom in the house was identical, which Rider assumed was on purpose to keep the minimalist look. They were all gray, with white marble, and white subway tiles. And all the towels in each bathroom were the same shade of medium gray.

"Did you get to my social media yet?" Thorn asked Jade. "It's getting late in the day and you know how my fans start to miss me."

Jade didn't stop. He continued toward the laundry room off the kitchen and said, "I'm going to do that right after I deal with these towels." Do you want anything special posted today?"

Thorn glanced up at the ceiling, thought for a second, then said, "Something inspirational today. I'm in that kind of a mood. Keep it simple and just repeat it on all my platforms. Maybe something about puppies and kittens. The sunrise could work, too. People always love *that*. Make them feel good."

"No problem," Jade said, as he left the room and his voice trailed off.

When he was gone, Rider asked, "Do you have to do a lot of social media work in your business?"

Thorn shook his head and said, "It never stops, and I'm not very good at it. I can barely figure out how to change the radio station in the car. Thankfully, Jade's excellent in that department. He handles all of my social media posts and no one knows it's not me."

This was one of the things about their film company that amazed Rider. They were known as one of the largest gay film producers in the adult entertainment industry and Thorn was the only one with a high public profile. Even though they were equal partners, very few people outside of their small circle even heard about Jade. In public, everything seemed to revolve around Thorn.

Rider had already checked out a few of Thorn's Tweets and Facebook status updates. They all sounded either sarcastic, inspirational, or downright pithy. He thought they'd all come from Thorn up until that moment. "Does Jade deal with all of your social media all the time?"

Thorn smiled. "Pretty much so. But don't tell anyone. My fans like to think it's really me they're replying to. You'd be amazed at how many women follow me on social media...all fans of gay porn. If they ever found out I don't have the slightest clue how to Tweet, Instagram, or Facebook, they'd never forgive me."

"Doesn't that make you feel a bit disingenuous sometimes?" Rider asked. Rider handled all of his own social media.

"Not at all," Thorn said. "Jade gives them what they want. He's so much nicer than I am. And that's the most important thing about social media. You tell them what they want and that's all they care about. Trust me on that. I might not be a genius with a computer, but I know how people think. If I were on social media I'd be posting photos of grumpy cat all day long and moaning about politics."

"I see," Rider said. He wasn't sure how he'd work this revelation into his article. He would probably leave it out completely, but it still gave him a deeper insight into Thorn.

"If you'll excuse me, I have to go out to the studio," Thorn said. "I'm auditioning a few new actors for an upcoming film and I want to get a few things organized before they arrive."

"No problem," Rider said. Thorn and Jade never seemed to stop working, not even on the weekend of their wedding. "You do keep busy around here." He would have thought that with the wedding that weekend, and the article they were doing, Thorn would have taken a few days off.

"Always working and always moving forward," Thorn said, as he turned to leave. "That's another reason why I don't have time for social media and I depend on Jade to deal with it. I like perfection, except there is no such thing as perfection. So I try for excellence instead. I didn't build a multi-million dollar studio because I took a lot of vacations."

"I'll have to remember that," Rider said. "I admire that kind of dedication."

"If you'd like to come down to the studio in a half hour, you're more than welcome," Thorn said. "It might be interesting for you to see how we audition the actors. I'm not sure how much of it you can use in the article, but you might find it worthy of mention."

Rider had a feeling Thorn was trying to get him to plug the film studio as much as possible in the article, without coming out and saying it directly. "I'll definitely come down," Rider said. He couldn't leave their business totally out of the article. "I don't want this article to read like an advertorial for a film studio, but I do have to mention the kind of work you do. I think readers will find that interesting."

"Excellent," Thorn said, turning to leave. "Just come down to the studio and my office is right off the main reception area. You can't miss it. There's no one else there today but me."

After he left, Rider reviewed his notes for a while, and then decided to go back outside and wait on the patio until it was time to walk down to the studio. Although he'd watched his fair share of porn, and he'd ruined a few cheap laptops in the process thanks to malware he'd picked up at porn sites, he'd never seen what went on behind the scenes in the adult entertainment industry.

On his way outside, he ran into Sandler in the dining room and said, "Did you have a productive morning? Did you officially change the name of the web site to *The Rainbow Times*?" Drew had finally spoken to Boris about the name change and Boris seemed fine with it. Rider also wanted to avoid any talk about sex. He still wasn't ready to get fucked again.

"Very productive," Sandler said. "The name was changed. Everything's going smoothly in LA and we should have a temporary page up online soon that people can view. It will inform readers that the web site is coming soon. Dequinn is working on the social media angle and press releases. I'll e-mail you a link later today and you can see for yourself." He walked over to where Rider was standing and grabbed his ass hard. "Wanna go back up to the room?"

Rider had never seen a man so needy. He smiled and took a few steps back. "I can't. I'm going to the studio now to watch a few actors audition for one of Thorn's upcoming films."

"Porn?"

"Yes."

"Can I come?"

"I don't see why not," Rider said. "You're working with me and I don't think Thorn would mind. Just remember we're there to observe. We're invisible."

"Okay," Sandler said. "I'll remember. I won't say a word."

A few minutes later, they entered Thorn's small film studio at the far end of the property and Rider glanced at three young men in the reception area. They were seated in different sections of the room waiting to be called into Thorn's office where they would audition. Rider found it interesting they all resembled Sandler, in looks, dress and manner. It was one of the oddest things he'd ever seen and he wondered if Sandler noticed it, too.

"Does anything look unusual to you in here?" Rider asked.

He smiled and shrugged. "Not really. It looks like any other average reception room. Reminds me of my dentist's office."

"I mean the guys," Rider said. They were all wearing sweaters, all had over-sized glasses, all looked as if they spent more time Tweeting than drinking. They were attractive, and Rider would have slept with any one of them at any given time. He just found it interesting that they all resembled each other so closely.

"They look like normal guys to me," Sandler said. "Why do you ask?"

"No reason in particular," Rider said. "I was just wondering." He couldn't come right out and say they all reminded him of Sandler.

They headed toward Thorn's office and knocked on the door. When Thorn told them to come in, he gestured to a few chairs next to his desk and said, "This is a nice surprise. Did Sandler come to audition, too? I think he's perfect for the upcoming movie."

Sandler's face turned red and he gulped.

"He's not here to audition, Thorn," Rider said. "He's working with me on the article and I thought it would be interesting for him to be here just to observe."

Thorn wasn't one of those people who take the word "no" lightly. He looked Sandler up and down again and said, "That's a shame. He'd be perfect for the part I'm thinking of."

"I'm sorry, Thorn," Rider said.

"Well now, hold on a minute, Rider," Sandler said. He looked at Thorn. "What do I have to do to audition?" He looked at Rider and shrugged. "I'm just curious."

Rider flung him a glance. "*You* want to audition for the film?"

Sandler shrugged. "Why not?"

"That's totally up to you," Rider said. "I just want you to know what you're getting into. Once something is on the Internet it's there forever. You fully understand that." He'd always believed there were certain times in life when we all reach a line, and if we cross that line there's no going back.

Sandler nodded. "Of course I do. I know the Internet well. I'm the one doing a lot of the tech work for the web site. This movie is something I've always wondered about doing, but I never thought I'd get the opportunity. I can promise you that I'm never going to run for President so I'm not worried about any scandals."

"Wonderful," Thorn said, before Rider could say another word. "I think you'll be perfect for this part. You go out now and get the other guys. Tell them to come in here and we'll get this audition started. It's getting late and I'd like to nap so I'll be fresh for the hayride tonight."

"Hayride?" Rider asked. No one had mentioned a hayride to him.

"Yes," Thorn said. "I thought Drew mentioned it to you." There's a fall festival in town tonight and we're all taking a horse and wagon over to Granny Smith's Bed and Breakfast. It's a tradition around here. You'll love it."

Rider forced a smile. "Oh, I'm sure I will. I can't wait." He was wondering what other insidious hells he would have to endure.

As Sandler escorted the three other young men into the office, Rider sat back in one of the chairs beside Thorn's desk and crossed his legs. As he reached into his jacket to get his small notebook and pen, Thorn sat down behind his desk and said, "Rather than audition you all privately, I'm going to keep this simple and do it all at once. Please remove all of your clothes, including your socks and underwear, and we'll get this over with quickly."

Rider had never seen four young men drop their pants so fast in his life. He set his notebook and pencil on the desk and leaned forward in the chair so he wouldn't miss a thing. While Thorn asked them all basic questions about where they were from and how much experience they'd had, Rider found it interesting that when they were all naked they all had similar body types. None of them were weight lifters, and yet they were thin and solid, with light patches of dark hair on their chests and abdomens. They all had hairy legs just like Sandler. If Rider hadn't known better, he might have mistaken them all for brothers.

The one physical similarity they didn't all share was between their legs. Each one had a slightly different penis. For some reason, Rider always found various penis sizes and shapes amusing, to the point where he categorized them in private. One of the guys had that chunky uncircumcised look, the tallest guy had one of those huge penis heads shaped like a fireman's hat, and the guy off to the right had an acorn head dick that reminded Rider of Boris's. They all had hair between their legs, too. They'd obviously trimmed their bushes for the audition, but they hadn't shaved everything.

The only one auditioning who truly stood out, so to speak, from the rest was Sandler. Thanks to his massive appendage, Thorn got up from the desk and walked across the room to examine it up close. He glanced back at Rider and smiled. "Now I see why you were making all that noise in bed. Dear God, I'm surprised you can even walk."

The other guys all glanced at Rider to see how he would respond. He didn't like being put on the spot that way, but there was nothing he could do but keep it light and carefree. He just smiled and said, "What can I say? I know what I'm doing."

Thorn glanced between Sandler's legs again and shook his head. "You certainly do."

Then Thorn stopped gawking at Sandler and he went back to his desk. He sat down and told them all to get erect, and then he explained to them he had to see them erect to know how they would appear on film. Rider had to admit he wasn't put off by Thorn's manner or tone when he explained everything to them. He kept it professional…almost clinical…about as professional as one can get in a situation like this and never once embarrassed or degraded any of them. It became apparent this was strictly business for Thorn and he wasn't interested in any of them in a sexual way. It almost seemed too clinical, to the point where Rider found nothing sexually arousing about it. Although Thorn never came out and said it aloud, he seemed more disinterested in them sexually than anyone Rider had ever known. He did, however, treat them all with great respect.

The only one who didn't grow erect was Sandler, and Rider started to feel sorry for him. His face had turned red again and Rider had a feeling he was experiencing a little performance anxiety. The other guys were so cool and laid back. Growing erect in public for them seemed so simple. Rider had a feeling they'd all taken enhancement pills for the audition. He'd read somewhere that most adult film actors did that sort of thing.

"Just give me a minute," Sandler said, as he stroked that huge flaccid penis. "I'm just a little nervous."

When Rider noticed one of the guys whisper something to another one about Sandler, and then snicker, Rider looked at Thorn and said, "Can I give him a little help. I think I know what to do. He'll be just fine." He felt sorry for the poor guy.

Thorn said, "Sure."

Rider got up from the chair, crossed the room, and put his arms around Sandler's shoulders. He whispered into his ear, "relax cutie, I'll get you hard," and then he rubbed his shoulders lightly and looked into his eyes. While the other guys watched, and Thorn remained seated at his desk, Rider then caressed the back of Sandler's head gently and kissed him on the lips. It was one of those long, deep kisses that lasted for a minute or two. And by the time he stopped kissing him, and he glanced down between Sandler's legs, his dick had grown to a full erection.

Sandler patted Rider's butt and said, "Thanks. You're the best, man."

The other guys just gaped at the size of him and said nothing at all. They didn't whisper, snicker, or comment now.

Thorn took one look at Sandler and said, "Okay, guys. You can all get dressed now. I've seen enough. Thank you all and I'll get back to you as soon as possible. I think I can use all of you in the future for something. I'll be in touch to work everything out." Then he looked at Rider and said, "Have you ever thought about acting in adult entertainment. I'm going to need someone just like you to play opposite the geek character, a slick, good-looking power bottom. I like opposites and you're perfect for Sandler. Besides, you're obviously already familiar with him."

Rider crossed back to the chair where he'd been sitting. He laughed and said, "Thank you, but I'm a journalist, not an actor."

"That's too bad," Thorn said. "You could be my next big power bottom."

"Well, thanks for that," Rider said, and then he picked up his notebook and pretended to be writing just to get off the topic. He already had enough issues with Drew. The last thing he needed was for Drew to find out he'd become a power bottom in gay porn.

CHAPTER TEN

After the guys put their clothes on, they filled out some kind of an application for employment and handed them to Thorn one at a time, including Sandler. Even though Rider had to admit he was a little surprised at Sandler's enthusiastic attitude about the prospect of doing gay porn, he said nothing to dissuade him and focused on taking a few more notes for the feature story.

"Well, that should take care of business today," Thorn said. He stood up, stretched his arms, and yawned. "Let's go back to the main house. I'm going to take a nap so I'm not exhausted tonight. If I don't, Jade will kill me."

"Does Jade nap with you?" Rider asked, as they crossed to the office door and headed into the reception area with Sandler in tow. He wanted to know everything about their relationship.

"Oh no," Thorn said. "He's not a nap person. He's never been much of a sleeper. I always joke around that it's his good old Yankee blood. He was actually born in New Hampshire, and his family dates back to before the revolution. He comes from good strong stock. No one in his family ever died before 90 years old, and never sick a day in their lives. My family stock is a different story. The men in my family never lived beyond 50 years old. And Jade has this ridiculous fear that I'm going to die young just like them. He insists that I nap daily for health reasons."

"Are you sick?" Rider asked.

"No," Thorn said, as he opened the door to head outside. "Jade is a fanatic. He schedules all kinds of medical appointments for me, and I've had all the tests you can give a person. Jade calls it preventative medicine, and I go along with it because it calms him down."

"It sounds kind of extreme," Rider said. He was finally beginning to get more insight into their relationship, which is what he wanted. He wasn't going to write personal details, but in order to generalize sometimes he knew he needed these details.

"It is extreme," Thorn said. He stopped near the entrance to the swimming pool and looked at Rider. "But that's what marriage is all about sometimes. You do things you normally wouldn't do to make things a little better for your spouse. Hell, I hate going to the doctor. But it makes Jade happy so I do it. He makes more than a few compromises for me so it's the least I can do for him. He's my entire life."

From what Rider could see so far, they both seemed genuinely concerned about making compromises. Jade basically said he did the same for Thorn. Of course, Jade did all that hard work around there and Thorn acted merely as the creative figurehead. Rider didn't say this aloud. He only smiled and said, "I think that's very nice, actually. I hope I can find that someday. You're both so devoted to each other."

Thorn turned to leave. Then he winked, and said, "If you're lucky you will."

As Thorn headed into the house so he could nap, Rider felt a hand on his behind and turned around to fine Sandler standing there with a big grin. "You're all horned up now after that audition, aren't you?"

Sandler squeezed him. "Oh yeah. That kiss you gave me did it."

"Maybe we should just take a nap," Rider said. "I'm not really looking forward to this hayride thing tonight and there's no way to get out of it."

"Okay," Sandler said. "Let's go upstairs and nap."

When they entered their room a few minutes later, it became apparent the last thing Sandler wanted to do was sleep. The moment the lock on the door clicked, he grabbed Rider by the waist and turned him around. Then he threw Rider down on the bed, climbed on top of him, and started kissing his neck.

Rider laughed and pushed his shoulders. "This isn't napping. Get off me."

Sandler pulled off his own shirt and said, "There's plenty of time for a nap."

Although Rider made a few more lame attempts to push him off, his legs were spread and up in the air. "I'm starting to think you're a sex manic or something. We really should put this into perspective. We're not in love, we're not interested in a relationship, and we're only having meaningless sex." Rider had had meaningless sex before…many times…but he'd never had it with the same person that many times.

"So what?" Sandler asked. "When the sex gets tired we'll stop. No one gets hurt."

"It just feels so wrong sometimes," Rider said.

"That's the best part about it. And you like it just as much as I do."

Rider put his arms around Sandler's shoulders and said, "You have a point there." He kissed his neck. "You smell good again today."

Sandler stopped kissing his neck and said, "I didn't put any body spray on at all and I've been perspiring."

"I know that," Rider said. He turned his head and inhaled the scent coming from his arm pit. "You smell just as good without it. It's okay for a man to smell like a man."

After he said that, Sandler got so turned on he stood up and removed the rest of his clothes in that awkward, gangly way he had. By the time he was naked, Rider had removed his clothes and he was resting on his back in the middle of the bed. While Sandler went over to the night stand to get the condom and lube, Rider lifted his legs, bent them at the knee, and spread them. Even though he knew this moment lacked the kind of intimacy he was beginning to crave, he couldn't deny he liked getting fucked by Sandler because Sandler liked doing it so much. It wasn't difficult for Rider. All he had to do was lie there and lift up his legs and wait. He would have enjoyed sucking Sandler's dick for a few minutes, but Sandler only seemed interested in fucking him.

145

Sandler climbed onto the bed and pulled the condom over his erection. He didn't remove his glasses…the only time he ever removed them was to sleep. Rider noticed that his dick was so big the condom only covered two thirds of it. He covered it with lube, and then reached between Rider's legs to lube him and probe with his fingers a few times. He could see that Sandler enjoyed what he was doing with his fingers and he looked into Rider's eyes the entire time he probed. When Rider threw his arms back and nodded, Sandler bit his bottom lip and inserted his middle finger as far as he could. Rider encouraged him by arching his back and spreading his legs even wider. Rider never knew if this was his weakest or strongest point with men, this inability to refrain from showing his own pleasure. Men knew how much he liked it and they knew they were in control the entire time, which often left him at a disadvantage when the sex was over.

When Sandler finally pulled his fingers out, he grabbed his dick and said, "Is this position okay?"

Rider nodded. "I think so. I want to try it this way." This was the first time Sandler had fucked him on his back. Each time before that Rider had either straddled his waist or Sandler had taken him from behind.

"If you want me to stop just let me know," Sandler said. "You can get on top of me again. I don't mind. Or I can just turn you over."

He ran his fingers down Sandler's hairy leg and said, "Just enter slowly and give me time to get used to you, cutie."

Sandler nodded and leaned forward. He pointed his erection between Rider's legs and entered him so slowly Rider didn't even have to grab the covers that time. As he went deeper there was a hint of discomfort, but it only lasted for a second or two. His heart started to race and his body grew hot all over. And by the time Sandler was all the way inside Rider was so surprised at how good it felt in this position he even joked about it.

"Tell me when you're inside," Rider said.

Sandler blinked. He couldn't get any deeper if he tried.

"I'm only joking," Rider said. He rubbed his leg again. "Everything's fine."

"No pain?"

Rider lifted his legs a little higher. "You feel wonderful. Stop worrying. Just don't get too rough. I don't want to make any noise. The whole house already thinks I'm a slut."

"You're not a slut, not by any means. You're adorable and you're one of the most honest people I've ever met. I think you're cool."

"Well that's debatable, depending on who you ask."

"Okay," Sandler said. "I'll be quiet."

"Good boy." He laughed and smacked his leg.

After he said that, it was as if he'd given Sandler permission to do whatever he wanted to do. He leaned forward and started fucking Rider slowly. Rider put his arms around Sandler's shoulders and they kissed. It wasn't the intimate kind of kissing he knew with Drew, where his eyes rolled back and he forgot what day of the week it was. In this case it was more sexual, and dirty, which Rider had come to realize wasn't the worst thing in the world. One of the issues he'd always had with Drew as a lover was that they'd never been totally honest with each other with regard to sex. He'd always felt as if they'd both held back, and only because they'd loved each other so much. It was as if they'd failed to express all their sexual needs and desires because they didn't want to offend each other...or shock each other. The sad truth was that Rider had never shown how much he enjoyed getting fucked, and Drew had never fucked him as hard and raw as he probably could have. The only time they even came close to honest sex was that one night recently in

Drew's house. This lack of communication was a flaw in their relationship that Rider didn't know how to fix, so he'd cheated with other guys to find out what was missing. And now he realized how wrong he'd been, and it was too late to do anything about it.

After they stopped kissing, Sandler started fucking him harder and faster. They remained in this position until Sandler said, "Hold on to my shoulders tightly. There's something I've always wanted to do. I'm close and I want to come this way."

Rider had no idea what he was talking about, but he grabbed his shoulders and nodded. "Do whatever you want. I'm close, too." He felt safe enough with Sandler to say that. He wouldn't have said that to Drew and he didn't even know why.

While he grabbed Sandler's shoulders, Sandler reached under his legs and lifted him up off the bed. When Sandler was standing, and Rider's legs were dangling over Sandler's arms, Sandler started fucking him again. He held the back of Sandler's neck and reached down to grab his own dick so he could jack it. He'd never been lifted off the ground and fucked this way before. He didn't even know it was possible for two men to fuck this way. And when he caught a glimpse of what they were doing in the mirror over the headboard, and he saw the way Sandler was fucking him, he pointed his toes and came so fast he didn't even realize he screamed.

Sandler came a moment later, and then he slowly walked back to the bed. As he lowered Rider on his back he remained inside and rested on top of him.

By that time they were both drenched in perspiration and the room wasn't even hot. Rider caressed the back of Sandler's head and said, "That was amazing. Where did you learn to do something like that?"

"I saw it once in a porn film," Sandler said. "I always wanted to do it."

"I never even knew I could do something like that."

"I'm sorry I'm all sweaty," Sandler said.

"I don't mind," Rider said. "We can shower after we nap."

"I'll pull my dick out in a minute," Sandler said.

"Take your time," Rider said. "I'm in no rush."

And then he closed his eyes and wondered why he'd never said anything that intimate or crude to Drew. After they had sex, they said they loved each other, and then they kissed and went into the bathroom to clean up separately. No once in all the time they'd been together did they ever just lie in their own sweat and enjoy it. They'd held so much back from each other because they loved each other so much they'd never fully been able to enjoy all the things they could have enjoyed during sex, and Rider started to wonder if that was the difference between sex with a casual fuck buddy and sex with a real lover.

CHAPTER ELEVEN

"Where the hell am I?" Rider asked. His head pounded and everything looked hazy.

"You fell off the wagon," Drew said.

"I *what?*"

"Literally," Drew said. "You had too much to drink at the festival and you *literally* fell off the wagon. The fraternity guys helped me get you back up here in the wagon to get you home, and we figured it would be safer if you slept it off out here."

"What fraternity guys?"

"The ones you got naked with in the hot tub."

"*Oh,* yeah." He started to remember. This was so unlike him. He rarely drank alcohol, and even if he did he rarely got drunk to the point of passing out.

Rider looked around and realized he was inside some kind of a wagon filled with hay. Drew was beside him and they were stretched out beneath several thick blankets. His mouth was dry, his temples pounded, and if he moved his head too fast he felt a sharp pain over his right eye.

He remembered going to the town festival in the wagon with everyone else, and then he remembered the frat boys. The bed and breakfast where they held the festival, *Granny Smith's*, also had a hostel out back where backpackers and students on budgets could spend the night inexpensively. On that particular weekend, a group of gay fraternity brothers had driven up to Vermont and they'd been invited to the festival. They'd brought their own cheap gin, they'd offered Rider a few drinks, and the last thing he remembered was jumping into the clothing optional hot tub with them and being passed around from one guy to the other.

"Did I do anything terrible?" Rider asked. "This is why I should never drink." He couldn't remember anything but being naked in the hot tub and all those big strong fraternity brothers spanking him.

Drew pointed to something on his jacket and smiled. "You won the dance contest."

Rider looked down and saw a blue ribbon pinned to his jacket. "I don't even remember dancing. I don't even know how to dance."

Drew laughed and said, "I'm not surprised. You were so drunk by then you could barely stand up."

"What happened after that?"

"I wouldn't know," Drew said. "After that you disappeared with that eager group of fraternity brothers and I didn't see you again until you staggered back to the wagon to leave with the rest of us. That's when you fell off the wagon. The fraternity brothers helped put you back inside, we all drove back to Thorn and Jade's place, and I've been in here with you ever since."

"What happened to Sandler?" Rider asked. He'd lost track of what happened to Sandler sometime between his fourth drink and removing his pants while the frat guys cheered him on.

"He decided to spend the night at the hostel," Drew said. "The last I saw of him he was making out with one of the fraternity brothers under a street lamp. Sorry about that. I guess Sandler is a little fickle when it comes to men."

"There's no need to apologize for *that*," Rider said. He figured if he didn't move his head too fast he wouldn't feel the pain. "That's the best news I've heard all weekend. Sandler and I are not a couple."

Drew's eyes opened wider. "You're not? You could have fooled me."

"No, we're not," Rider said. "I wasn't sure how to get rid of him. He's very aggressive sometimes, and very needy."

"Here I thought you two were the next new gay power couple," Drew said.

Rider detected a hint of sarcasm in his tone and said, "Oh, please. He's a great guy. He's going to be great for the web site. But the only thing between us was sex. Plain and simple."

"Isn't that convenient for you," Drew said, without any expression at all that time.

He definitely heard the sarcasm in that comment. "I'm not apologizing for anything I did with Sandler," Rider said. "I'm not with anyone, I'm not in a relationship, and that's not cheating."

Drew smiled. "I never said it was cheating. You sound so guilty. You're a grown man and you're free to do whatever you want. In fact, I encourage it. Men like you shouldn't be tied down to one person. You *should* be free to do whatever you want."

"Then why does it feel like I cheated," Rider said. "I know I didn't. It just feels as if I did."

Drew shrugged and said, "You'll have to figure that one out on your own. I'm afraid I can't help you there."

"What time is it anyway?"

Drew glanced at his watch and said, "It's a little after five in the morning."

He spoke with such a calm, relaxed voice Rider wanted to close his eyes and go back to sleep. "Did you spend the entire night here with me, in this wagon, under these covers?"

"Yes, I did," Drew said. "I couldn't let you sleep here alone, and no one could get you back into the house."

"Are you cold?" Rider asked. "He pulled the cover up to their necks and rested his head on Drew's chest.

"No, not at all," Drew said. "These covers are actually very warm, and it's still mild outside for this time of year."

"Thank you for doing that," Rider said. "You didn't have to. You could have let me sleep here alone all night."

"There's no need to thank me. You're the only one who can write this article and I wasn't going to take any chances. My decision was based purely on the success of this new web site."

Rider's hand slowly went down Drew's torso. It stopped at Drew's crotch and Rider slowly unzipped his pants.

"What are you doing?" Drew asked.

"I thought I would thank you properly," Rider said. Even though his temples were still pounding, and his mouth still dry, he hadn't been this turned on by anyone in a long time.

Drew smacked his hand and pulled up his zipper. "Stop that."

"I only wanted to give you a little morning blowie," Rider said.

Drew laughed. "I think it's time to get up."

"No," Rider said. "I want to talk about something and I want to do it right now."

Drew pushed the covers off them and turned to get up. "Well I don't want to talk about anything right now. I want to go back into the house, climb into my nice comfortable bed, and sleep for a few more hours. I think you can find your way into the house alone from this point on."

Rider tried to stand up, but his legs were still a little wobbly. As Drew stood to climb out of the wagon, he grabbed his arm and said, "Don't I even get a kiss good-bye."

Drew turned and flung him a glare. "No, you don't get a kiss. It's not that easy, Rider. That's not how things work in life. I'm not your fuck buddy. I'm your ex. I'm the one you were in a relationship with and I'm the one you cheated on."

He released his arm and looked down at his lap. "You're never going to let me forget that, are you?"

Drew threw his leg over the side and jumped down from the wagon. "I don't hold it against you, Rider. You can't help yourself. It's in your nature to cheat. I've thought about it a lot and I've come to the conclusion that some people simply can't help themselves. And you're one of them."

"That's not true," Rider said. "And if you'd get off your high horse and you'd let me explain maybe you'll feel differently. You're the *only* person I was ever in a relationship with, and I was too young to understand what I was doing. Unlike you, my life didn't come with an instruction manual."

Drew looked up at the sky. "And letting every guy that came along get into your pants was the solution?"

"It wasn't like that at all," Rider said. "It was only a few guys, not every guy that came along."

"A few too many," Drew said.

"Possibly," Rider said. "I regret that now. But I don't think it's totally fair to hold it against me for the rest of my life, or to slut shame me forever. I've admitted I was wrong. I've apologized more times than I can count. I'm not sure what else I can do to please you."

Drew took a deep breath and exhaled. "I need to go inside. There's a wedding tomorrow and it's going to be a long day. I'll see you later this morning. You should go inside before the sun comes up and people see you here. It's not very becoming. You also have an article to write, and I'm starting to worry that it's not going to be very interesting. So far you're the only one who seems to be having any fun at all around here, thanks to Sandler and his unusually large penis."

"Oh, you heard about his penis."

Drew rolled his eyes. "Who hasn't? Thorn's been talking about it since Sandler auditioned and he can't seem to get the image out of his head. I have to give you credit. It's not everyone who can handle a man with a penis the size of a baseball bat. I'm sure you're quite good at it."

"That's an exaggeration," Rider said. "It's not a baseball bat. And stop being so damn smug and judgmental. You have no right to slut shame me that way, not anymore."

"I have no idea what you're talking about. I'm only stating a fact."

"Oh yes you do know what I'm talking about," Rider said. "You're trying to make me feel guilty and I didn't do anything wrong this time. You always do that."

"What I don't understand is why you even care so much," Drew said.

"Because I do care," Rider said. "I care a lot. I never stopped caring."

"I still like you," Drew said. "I'm not mad at you anymore. We're working together again and I thought everything was fine."

"There you go again," Rider said. "You're pacifying me as if I were a child."

"I am not," Drew said. "You're getting hysterical now. You'll wake everyone."

"I am not hysterical," Rider said. "You're just saying I'm hysterical because that's what you do."

"What do you mean?"

"That's what you always do," Rider said. "You condescend, and treat me as if I'm a hysterical gay man because you're the top and I'm the bottom."

"Now you're really going off on a tangent," Drew said. "And I'm going back inside to sleep. There's no talking to you when you're like this. You're not making sense."

"If I am a little hysterical, and I'm not saying I am, it's because I have good reason to be," Rider said. "I'm not perfect, and neither are you."

Then Drew turned and headed toward the house, with his hands in his pockets and his head down. This was typical of Drew. Rather than face a problem head on, he tended to walk away from it and pretend it didn't exist.

"Go on, walk away," Rider said. "But we're not finished yet. We're going to talk this out if I have to tie you to a tree to get you to listen."

Drew sent him a backward glance and smiled. "Get some sleep, Rider. You're far too pretty to have dark circles beneath your eyes."

Rider smiled and spoke with a softer voice. "Thanks again for staying here with me. I don't know what I'd do without you in my life. I'd do the same for you. I'd do anything for you."

"I know that," Drew said. "And that's exactly why I stayed. Even though it's painful sometimes, someone needs to watch out for the silly people of the world because the truth is I don't know what I'd do without you either."

Rider wanted to run after him, but he couldn't get his legs to move that fast. He could barely get them to move. He wanted to get a few things out in the open about their relationship, things that had been bothering him since they'd split up. However, he decided to let things rest for the time being. At least they'd talked about something of importance for once. The best he could do was go back into the house and sleep his hangover off, so he crawled to the edge of the wagon, with the blue ribbon he'd won in the dance contest dangling from his jacket, and slowly worked his way over the side.

*****

162

At ten in the morning, Rider walked into the dining room and found Sandler sitting at the table in the same clothes he'd been wearing the night before. He was shoving a buttered muffin into his mouth and staring at a big ripe banana. They were the only two in there, so Rider walked over to the buffet to get some black coffee and asked, "What happened to me last night?"

Sandler swallowed and said, "I think I met a guy I really like. His name is Brent and he lives in New York. I'm seeing him again today before he goes back home."

Rider carried the coffee to the table and sat down across from him. He'd taken aspirin and his head didn't hurt as much anymore, but some noises still sent chills through his body. "That's nice," he said. "I'm talking about me. What did I do? I never drink that way. I can't remember a thing."

"Oh, you had fun," Sandler said. "And you won the dance contest."

"So I've heard."

"Those guys really had fun passing you around, too," Sandler said. "They had a blast spanking you."

163

"Oh," Rider said. At least that explained the red marks on his bottom that morning. "Did I have sex with any of them? Please tell me I didn't have sex with all of them."

"Well, that depends on what you call sex," Sandler said.

He could see he had to be blunt. "Did any of them fuck me?"

"No," Sandler said. "I was there the whole time. You didn't have sex with any of them. The only thing that happened was they passed you around the hot tub naked and they spanked you. After that, you fell asleep and the guys set you down on a lounge chair next to the hot tub. I think more would have happened, but you were so drunk the guys left you alone. Then Drew found you passed out and he dried you off and got you dressed."

"Drew dressed me?" Drew hadn't mentioned that to him.

Sandler nodded and reached for the banana. "He dressed you, helped carry you to the wagon, and stayed with you the entire time to make sure you were okay."

As Rider was about to reply, Drew walked into the dining room with Jade and smiled. "How is everyone feeling this morning?" He looked at Rider first, as if he expected Rider to moan into his coffee.

Rider squared his back, and said, "Good morning. I've never felt better."

CHAPTER TWELVE

After he finished his third cup of black coffee, Rider stood and said, "I'm going back to my room to work on the feature a little. I need some substance for this article." He didn't feel like talking or smiling. The hangover was subsiding but his eyes were still heavy and he wanted to get a few things written down while they were still fresh. He still wasn't totally certain where the main angle of this story would lead him, and that bothered him a lot more than it should have. No one else seemed to care about the quality of the feature or the web site. The rest of them…including Drew…seemed more focused on the clickbait appeal and getting as many hits as they could.

Drew was sitting at the head of the table reading e-mails on his phone. He glanced up and said, "Don't forget the wedding is at four o'clock this afternoon."

Rider frowned. "How could I? Who gets married at four o'clock in the afternoon?"

"According to Jade, Thorn's Aunt Betty wanted it to be held at that time because she never misses tea time. And she doesn't want it to interfere with her five o'clock nap. She thought it would be a novelty to have a tea time wedding," Drew said, with a hint of snark in his voice. "So Jade will be running around all day today preparing for his own wedding and Aunt Betty's high tea."

"Jade does a lot of running around from what I can see," Rider said. "I have a feeling if I really wrote this article the way I see things happening around here, Thorn wouldn't be too pleased. Aunt Betty might even hit me with her purse."

Drew sent him a stare. "Then don't. This feature has to be light, and positive. We're creating an example here for other gay men. And in case you haven't noticed, Jade loves doing what he's doing. In fact, I have never seen another gay man so devoted to his husband as Jade is devoted to Thorn. He absolutely adores him. And frankly, I'm not sure I ever will see that kind of adoration again. They have a balance that I'm afraid I'll never see in my lifetime, a good, solid balance that keeps them together."

He had a feeling Drew was throwing a little shade in his direction, so he smiled and said, "You never know, Drew. You might just get lucky someday and someone will sweep you off your feet and adore you just as much. Or, since you like to control things so much, you can get a dog that will obey your every order and command."

Drew rolled his eyes and looked at his phone again. "I highly doubt that. I don't think I have time to devote to a dog, and I tend to be attracted to silly, frivolous men who thrive on being obtuse. Besides, from what I've learned so far in life that kind of thing is highly overrated anyway."

"On that note, I'll go upstairs and work," Rider said. He didn't want to argue with him again, and he knew Drew was sending him signals.

"You do that," Drew said, without looking up. "Have a nice day."

"I'll do my best."

A few minutes later, when Rider sat down at a desk in his room and opened his laptop, he tried as hard as he could to embellish the story of Jade and Thorn. He even went to a few web sites that published nothing but the most idiotic gay news, about shallow gay couples dealing with shallow events that didn't even make sense half the time. He wanted to check out the way the articles were written. Most of the headlines didn't even work with the stories. Pure clickbait designed only to get hits and to trick people into reading about nothing of importance.

While he read the articles he made faces and wondered how these so-called journalists who wrote that garbage ever found jobs working on news items in the first place. His old journalism professors in college would have gagged. They truly would have believed the end of days was approaching soon based on that kind of journalism. The way the articles were written, with one hideous cliché after another, not to mention the grammatical issues, made Rider wonder if these so-called writers had even gone to grade school. But more than that, there didn't seem to be any objectivity whatsoever. These articles weren't only slanted in one direction, they were slanted on purpose to sway and control public opinion with the kind of peer pressure people thought they'd left behind in junior high school.

He worked for the next four hours building a story around a successful, middle aged gay couple who had found a balance that kept them going. He mentioned they'd made all their money in adult entertainment, but didn't make that the focus. Although he knew this wasn't the kind of simple clickbait story the other commercial gay presses

169

published, he tried not to use words that were too complicated, and he kept the sentences short and easy on purpose. He figured if he could focus on the intimacy of their relationship, and all the years they'd spent building it, he couldn't go wrong. The only problem was that he still hadn't found a distinct angle that would make it different from everything else out there that had already been done before. But most of all, he couldn't find the emotion.

By the time he finished showering and dressing for the wedding, it was almost four o'clock and Sandler came rushing into the room in a panic. "I don't have much time. Can I use the bathroom now? I have to get downstairs and take photos."

Rider was wearing his navy blue suit with the extra tight pants. "Sure, I'm finished. Where were you all day?"

"I went over to say goodbye to Brent," Sandler said. "His bus leaves in a half hour. And I guess I got sidetracked. We wound up in bed for most of the day."

Rider headed for the door. "Well at least you had fun. I'm glad you met someone."

Sandler pulled off his shirt and said, "He's coming out to LA in a few weeks. His brother lives in East LA. I really like him, and he's almost as good as you are in bed. He's just not as experienced, he's not as willing to do *anything*, and he hasn't had as many men as you've had."

Rider laughed. He had a feeling this would only be a passing fling for Sandler, but he didn't say it aloud. "Well, thank you, I think. I'm going downstairs now. I'll see you in a few minutes." He found it interesting they all thought he'd had so many men. He always wondered just how many men were considered too many, and who the hell made those rules.

On his way downstairs, he realized he truly was happy for Sandler. He'd been a little worried that Sandler might want more from their relationship…more than Rider was prepared to give.

He found Drew in the living room gazing at the Christmas decorations. Jade must have put up a few more smaller Christmas trees that day, and there seemed to be more elaborate strands of pre-lit garland hanging almost everywhere he looked. If it didn't twinkle, it sparkled. If it wasn't gold, it was silver. The room was starting to resemble the inside of a Christmas shop in a tourist town he used to visit every summer. The only thing missing was a big gold chair and Santa waiting for someone to sit on his lap.

When Drew saw him enter, he turned and asked, "Is Sandler coming down soon? I want to get photos of everything."

"He'll be down right away," Rider said. "I just talked to him."

"I'm sure you did," Drew said. "You've been enjoying him."

"Don't be nasty," Rider said. "You know damn well there's nothing serious between us. I worked all day alone and Sandler spent the day with his new found love, some guy in that fraternity named Brent."

"Well, I'm sorry for your loss," Drew said. "I'm sure you'll find another man, or two, or three."

"Don't be sorry. I'm very happy for Sandler. I hope he finds what I never could find in a relationship. Something good, without judgment." He said that last part on purpose, in retaliation for the slut-shaming remark.

Drew made a face. "Just as long as he's here in time I don't care where he spent the afternoon."

"As I said, he'll be right down."

"Good," Drew said. "Jade and Thorn are upstairs getting dressed, the judge is in the dining room sampling the food, and Aunt Betty is still in her room sulking."

"Why?"

"Evidently, she wanted to give Thorn away," Drew said. "She wanted to walk him down the aisle, the traditional way, and Jade wouldn't hear any of it. He refused to back down this time. He doesn't want this to be a traditional wedding. That's why he didn't invite anyone other than us. He wants this wedding uncomplicated and he's not backing down."

"Good for him," Rider said.

"I was worried for a minute," Drew said. "I thought Thorn might buckle and let Aunt Betty have her way. But he finally agreed with Jade and now she's up in her room sulking."

"Let her sulk," Rider said. "It's about time someone put her in her place."

As the rest of the day unfolded, Rider noticed there was nothing traditional about this wedding at all. Everyone seemed to gather in the living room around the same time without planning it. While Sandler stood off to the side to get photos, Aunt Betty quietly sat down on a hard plastic Eames chair, with her jaw and fists clenched, beside the fireplace without saying a word. Drew and Rider stood next to the sofa, and Jade and Thorn followed the judge to the fireplace. They wore formal dark suits and ties, and thankfully they didn't match. Someone had turned on soft classical music that filtered through the room to add just enough atmosphere to make this disorganized event a little more special.

When everyone was situated and the judge began the ceremony, Thorn and Jade exchanged a look and a smile. They seemed to forget there was anyone else in the room. Even though Rider didn't know them well, and he hadn't planned to get emotional that afternoon, he had this feeling that something more important was happening than he'd expected. The magnitude of the entire ceremony…the act of marriage itself…hit him hard, especially when Jade and Thorn began to read vows they'd written themselves. And by the time the judge pronounced them married, Rider felt a sting in his eye that left him wondering why he'd never taken anything this seriously before in his life.

While Jade and Thorn kissed, Drew turned to Rider and said, "Are you crying?"

"No," Rider said. He wanted to wipe his eye, but didn't dare do it at that moment. He'd never liked showing emotion.

"Yes you are," Drew said.

"Well, maybe a little," Rider said. "I guess I didn't expect this to hit me so hard. I've been to hundreds of straight weddings before and I never felt a thing. I wrote articles about same sex marriage for a long time. I shouldn't be this emotional, but this is the first time I've ever seen a gay couple get married in such a personal, intimate way. It's hard to explain. For some reason, this seems different."

Drew put his arm around his waist and said, "I know exactly how you feel."

"I feel like an idiot," Rider said, wiping his other eye. "This is work. I shouldn't be feeling anything right now. I should be objective."

"Well, at least I know you're human," Drew said, pulling him closer. "I've been worried about that for quite some time."

"I'm not sure if that's a compliment or an insult," Rider said, "but I'm too happy for them to care."

As Aunt Betty stood up to hug Thorn, the judge turned to head back to the dining room to sample a few more small potatoes topped with caviar and sour cream.

Jade turned around and said, "Let's go into the dining room now. I'll open the champagne and we'll have a toast. Aunt Betty naps at five o'clock."

Drew removed his hand from Rider's back and said, "This is ridiculous. He's been doing everything around here all day. The man hasn't stopped working for a minute. I'm going in there and I'll open the champagne and make the toast so he can enjoy what little he has left of his wedding day."

As Drew turned to leave, Aunt Betty started to complain about the champagne. She stomped her foot and said, "I don't want champagne. I want tea. This is tea time, after all. And I don't think there's a thing in there that I can eat."

Jade threw her an exasperated sigh and forced a smile. "I'll get your tea, Aunt Betty. And I'm sure we'll find something for you in the kitchen. I think we have nachos."

Rider noticed that Thorn wasn't even paying attention. He was off in the corner now talking to Sandler about something. If Aunt Betty had been Rider's aunt, and she'd been treating his husband the way she was treating Jade, Rider would have told her go make her own damn tea.

Jade just smiled and turned toward the dining room, moving quickly the way he normally did. However, when he reached the doorway that led into the dining room, he stopped, grabbed his chest, and fell over sideways without saying a word.

Rider was watching him so he ran over first. When he kneeled down beside him and saw that his lips had turned gray, he looked up and shouted, "Someone call 911. I think he's had a heart attack."

While Rider turned Jade on his back and opened his collar, Thorn rushed over and kneeled down beside him.

"Is he okay?" Thorn asked. His face had turned pale and his expression exuded panic.

"I don't know," Rider said. He'd taken a course in CRP once in college that he never thought he'd have to use. "Did someone call 911?"

Sandler was standing over them. "I just called. They're on their way."

Rider started to perform CPR on Jade, and Drew and the judge rushed into the room to see what had happened. Rider heard them but he didn't look up. He remained focused on Jade until the EMTs arrived and took over for him. They found a pulse and went to work immediately. So much happened so fast that Rider lost track of the details, and the next thing he knew they were carrying Jade out the front door on a stretcher.

At first, they wouldn't allow Thorn to ride along in the ambulance. They claimed it was some kind of insurance rule, but Thorn refused to back down. He literally pushed them out of the way and said he would buy the damn ambulance and the hospital if he had to. Then he climbed into the ambulance, sat down beside Jade, and dared them to stop him from riding along. And when they saw how serious he was, they decided to back down and break the rules that one time.

Rider, Drew, and Sandler followed the ambulance in Thorn's car to a community hospital about a half hour away. Drew drove because he said Rider would break the law. And he was right, too. When Rider was in an emergency situation like this he didn't care about turn signals or anything other than getting to where he was going. So Rider sat in the passenger seat and tugged on his seatbelt. Sandler sat in the back and gazed out the window.

It seemed to take forever to get to the hospital, and all the roads were those empty, nervous two lane affairs, with hills, valleys, and sharp curves. Rider was so used to freeways and boulevards he didn't find the trip to the hospital relaxing in the least. If anything it set him more on edge. At least they didn't lose track of the ambulance, which turned out to be a good thing. They had no idea where they were going and if they had lost ambulance they might have wound up in Canada.

CHAPTER THIRTEEN

"I'm going out for a long walk," Sandler said. "I need some fresh air."

As he watched Sandler stand up and lope toward the front door with his head down, Rider set his coffee cup on the table and said, "That's a good idea. I may do that later today."

It was one of those bright, crisp blue-green Vermont mornings that smelled of dried leaves and smoky fireplaces. The weather person was predicting light snow that night and the heating system in the renovated barn had been working overtime all morning. Rider glanced at the head of the table to Drew and asked, "Where's Thorn?"

"He's up in his room sleeping," Drew said. "The doctor gave him a sedative last night and I forced him to take it before he went to bed."

"Good idea," Rider said, and then he picked up his coffee cup and sighed aloud.

When they'd arrived at the hospital last evening, they'd pulled up right behind the ambulance and jumped out of the car to see what was happening with Jade. It only took one quick glance for Rider to know. Of course they wheeled Jade into the emergency room, and then back to one of the small rooms to work on him. The doctor and a few nurses ran to his side. They did the best they could do, given the circumstances. The EMTs had done the best they could do for him. Unfortunately, Jade had taken his final breath on route to the hospital and there was nothing anyone could have done to save him by the time he reached the emergency room.

Even though they barely knew Jade and Thorn, Drew took care of all the details with the hospital while Rider sat with Thorn in a small waiting room. Rider kept patting Thorn on the back, without saying anything. There didn't seem to be any words to offer that would bring him comfort or wisdom. Thorn, dazed and confused, sat there in his wedding suit staring down at the floor without moving his head. He responded to questions with a nod or a gesture, but it was as if he'd temporarily lost the ability to speak. The only thing he kept repeating was the same sentence: "I never thought my wedding day would be the worst day of my life."

Of course Rider knew he was in shock. He couldn't think of anything plausible to say, at least not without sounding disingenuous, so he simply nodded and patted his back until it was time to leave.

"Did Thorn say if there are going to be any services, or a memorial?" Rider asked.

"As far as I know, there's not going to be anything right now," Drew said. "According to Thorn, they both have wills and each one of them made it clear, in writing, what they wanted done when they pass away. Jade didn't want any religious ceremony or burial. He didn't have any family, other than Thorn. He wanted cremation and if Thorn wants to do some kind of memorial service at a later date that's up to him to do at his own discretion."

"What about the feature we're doing?" Rider asked. Even though he hated to exploit the situation, he knew he had one of the most moving stories he might ever write. In ways he'd never imagined, it tied up all the pragmatic work he'd done with same sex marriage. It was almost too perfect and bittersweet at the same time.

"I've been thinking about that," Drew said. He sat back in his chair and rubbed his eyes. "I think we should go forward with it, as long as Thorn agrees. I'll talk to him later and see what he thinks."

"I agree," Rider said. "I don't want to exploit them. If anything I'd like to make this a tribute to Jade."

Drew frowned. "And no one else will do it," he said. "I've already checked out the other news outlets and they've reported Jade's death, but with headlines that are designed as clickbait. Some quasi journalists are focusing only on the fact that Jade and Thorn own a large gay porn studio."

"I figured that would happen," Rider said.

"That's why I want our feature to be completely different," Drew said. "Hell, just the concept alone of a young gay widower is something totally new to everyone. I think it's our job to show just how much legalized same sex marriage has changed life for gay people. And I want to do it first before those straight actors, writers, and producers get a chance to appropriate us again."

"There have always been gay widowers," Rider said. "You know that as well as I do."

"Not officially or legally," Drew said. "In the past when marriage wasn't legal we were never taken as seriously as straight couples. *Never.* If one of us died, they would say we lost our 'friend.' Or they would say we lost our lifelong 'companion.' And in the obituary the surviving partner/spouse would be listed at the very end, below family and distant relatives, in the most insignificant way. I've seen it before too many times. Officially, we could never actually refer to ourselves as widows or widowers. We were never allowed that basic respect. And I think that's significant and I'm hoping that Thorn will agree."

"I can't argue that point," Rider said. "I'll mention it in the article in more detail."

"Good. I think that's important."

"I hope I can make this really good," Rider said. "I know Jade wasn't an activist and he shunned most things public and let Thorn deal with it. There was nothing outrageous or stereotypical about him either. But he's the quiet soul behind the scenes, just like the rest of us, who lived his life the best way he knew how. I'm just going to tell the truth, with dignity and decorum. I think Jade would have liked that."

"I'm sure you'll do a good job," Drew said. He stood up from the table and stretched. "I'm going to go upstairs and check on Aunt Betty now."

"How's *she* doing?" Rider asked. When they returned to the house last night and Aunt Betty heard what had happened to Jade, she nearly lost her balance and fell sideways. Then she slowly went down on her knees and let out a moan that sent a million shivers through Rider's body.

"She's still really shaken up," Drew said. "I'm kind of surprised. I didn't think she got along with Jade."

"Well, he did a lot for her," Rider said. "He never once complained about it. I feel awful leaving tomorrow. I know I'm supposed to be objective and this is work, but I feel so invested already and I didn't even realize it was happening."

Drew turned toward the kitchen and said, "We can't change our plans. We have to get back to LA and get this web site launched. And the sad truth is there's really nothing we can do for Thorn now. This is one of those things he'll have to figure out on his own. I don't envy him at all."

"Let's take Thorn out to dinner tonight," Rider said. "I think it will be good to get him out of the house."

"I'll see what I can do," Drew said. "He has to eat something today."

After Drew left to go upstairs to check on Aunt Betty, Rider went into the living room to check in with the office and go through his inbox. He already knew how he would write the feature and he wasn't worried about finding a focus anymore. He'd found the emotion, more than he ever thought he would find. He replied to an e-mail from Boris to let him know what was happening. Boris had already heard the news about Jade and he wanted to know how the feature was going. Rider replied with a few short lines that everything was moving forward and he would talk to him when he returned to LA tomorrow.

It wasn't easy to focus on work that day for a variety of reasons. The doorbell kept ringing and the house began to fill up with flower arrangements and the obligatory gift baskets people send in condolence. Rider didn't have to deal with any of that. Although she was still walking around as if she couldn't believe what had happened to Jade, Aunt Betty seemed to take pleasure in answering the door and checking out all of the deliveries. From what Rider could see, she frowned at the fresh fruit baskets, but her eyes seemed to light up whenever a gift basket with cheese arrived. It was an unusual day and the entire house took on that strange feeling that something tragic had happened, as if the house itself was in mourning for Jade.

When Sandler returned from his long walk, he went up to their room and worked on a few technical issues with the web site. He said he had to go through photos, and he used tech words and phrases that Rider didn't understand...and never would understand. Drew spent most of the day either working in his room or checking on Thorn.

At seven o'clock that evening, it seemed everyone had had enough silence. Rider stood up and smiled when Drew and Thorn entered the living room. Last he'd heard, Drew still wasn't sure if Thorn would join them for dinner at a restaurant. "I'm glad you're joining us, Thorn," Rider said. "I know we don't know each other very well, but I'm worried about you. Is there anything I can do?"

Thorn was wearing a black mock turtleneck and dark jeans. His eyes were red and his skin still had an ashen look. "I'm okay," he said. "I'm glad you were all here this weekend. It didn't make anything easier, but it did give me a diversion. You know, I've heard that trite expression that life can change in the blink of an eye but I never truly understood what it meant until now. That really is how it happens, though: in the blink of an eye."

Drew and Rider exchanged a look. Rider could see Thorn was still distraught and probably in shock. He changed the subject and asked, "Where's Aunt Betty? I made reservations for five. I assumed she'd be coming with us."

Thorn smiled for the first time since he'd found out Jade was dead. "Oh, don't worry about her. I checked in on her a few minutes ago and she's in her room with four gift baskets of cheese and she'll be fine. She never was big on going out to restaurants. Trust me, we'll have a much easier time without her complaining about the wait staff."

They went to a small local restaurant on the edge of town that seemed to be a mix of townies and tourists. The tourists dressed trendier, and had condos at the big ski resort on the mountain. The entire place smelled of meat and garlic, and had low ceilings, dim lights, and the walls were all dark brown wood. There were narrow booths up front with tall wooden benches. In the back, there were dark brown tables with captain chairs. In spite of the fact that this was considered one of the best restaurants in town, the specials were written on a blackboard in multi-colored chalk and there were so many people you couldn't pass through without rubbing up against someone. This was really one of the best parts of Vermont that Rider had noticed since he'd been there. The people there knew how to eat as well as in any French restaurant in LA, but they did it on hard wooden benches, wearing plaid shirts and jeans, with stainless steel utensils that didn't match.

The moment they entered and the locals saw Thorn, they were all escorted back to the best table in the house and treated as if they were the only people there that night. Locals came over and offered their condolences, while tourists watched and listened and wondered. So many people came over to their table in a show of respect, Rider found it fascinating and amazing. They obviously knew what Thorn and Jade did for a living, and yet no one seemed to judge them for producing gay porn. There was nothing puritanical about these people. That was another positive aspect of this little Vermont town for Rider. On the surface, though quaint and conservative in appearance, the people who made up the town didn't seem concerned about anything other than the loss Thorn had suffered. He was their neighbor, nothing more or less.

When it was time to pay, Drew pulled out his wallet and insisted Thorn was his guest that night. He said he would charge it to his business account, which was the least he could do after Thorn had welcomed them into their home so easily. Drew blinked when the waitress refused his credit card and told him the owner would not take any money from them that night. Then the owner himself came over to their table and spoke so highly of Jade it brought tears to Thorn's eyes.

On the way out to the car, Drew said, "I'm sorry, Thorn. I thought it would be good for you to get out tonight. I had no idea everyone would come over to the table that way and bring it all up again."

"The food was great," Sandler said. "There's that."

Thorn wiped his eyes and smiled. "I'm okay. It was good to get out. I actually feel better now. This is why Jade and I moved all the way up here, for the people. It's the most wonderful little place we ever came across and I loved hearing them talk so well about Jade. This was better for me than any sedative out there. I think I'll sleep tonight, at least for a while. I fall into these deep sleeps for an hour or two, and when I wake up it still hasn't dawned on me that he's gone forever. I forget for a moment. Then it hits and I remember, and it hits hard, so damn hard. I can't even explain the feeling."

Sandler took a step back and put his hands in his pockets. He clearly didn't know what to say and no one could blame him.

Rider opened the door for Thorn and said, "I know what you mean, Thorn, about this town. I came here thinking I was going to the end of the world, and I now know exactly what you mean. I hate to leave tomorrow."

Thorn turned and put his palms on Rider's shoulders. He looked him in the eye and said, "Well, you have to leave. Of course you're welcome to come back any time you want, but you have to go back to LA and write the best damn feature about Jade that was ever written."

Rider nodded. "You know I'll do the best I possibly can. And if Drew agrees, it's going to be a three part feature, not just a one-time deal." He'd been thinking about this and he hadn't even run it by Drew yet.

Drew shrugged. "I'm fine with that," he said. "In fact, I'm kind of sorry I didn't think of it first. I love it."

Then Thorn hugged him and said, "Thank you. You have no idea what this means to me. And there's no one else I would trust to do it but you guys."

"Why?" Rider asked.

"You remind me of the way Jade and I were twenty years ago," Thorn said. "It wasn't easy for us in the beginning either. You'll figure it out."

CHAPTER FOURTEEN

After they said goodnight to Thorn, Drew and Sandler headed upstairs to their rooms so they could get to bed a little earlier than usual. They were all heading back to LA in the morning and it would be a long day. Rider hadn't even packed yet, which wasn't usual for him. Whenever he went someplace he really liked, packing too soon made him feel as if he was rushing to get home, especially when he wanted to spend more time in the place he was visiting. And that night, if he'd been given a choice, he would have left everything in LA to move to Vermont permanently.

As Drew and Sandler climbed the stairs, Rider said, "I'll be up in a few minutes. I'm not tired yet and I'd like to read a little."

Drew looked down at him and said, "You can read in bed. Tomorrow will be a busy day. You should get some sleep."

Rider looked up and smiled. "I just want some quiet time, is all. I'll be up in a minute. This hit me hard."

Drew's eyebrow went up and he appeared somewhat surprised. Even though he didn't say anything, Rider suspected Drew was wondering why he needed quiet time. On any given occasion Rider tended to place himself in situations where he was surrounded by other people. If he was alone for too long he tended to get an uneasy feeling in his stomach and he'd never been sure why that happened. Oh, he'd always marveled at those people who could go to the movies alone, or even eat in a restaurant alone. They always appeared so tall and erect and proud of their solitude, showing all their self-confidence without even realizing it. Drew was that kind of person. He didn't need other people around to do anything. There had been times when Rider and Drew had been a couple when Rider wondered if Drew *ever* needed other people around.

After they left him on the first floor, Rider went into the keeping room and sat down in one of the Eames chairs near the fireplace. They'd had all the fireplaces in the old barn converted to gas, and with a flip of one switch on a small remote control he had the perfect fire going. When Jade had decorated the living room for the wedding with a Christmas theme, he'd set all the lights to the Christmas trees and garland on automatic timers and the entire room was glowing in multi-colored lights. On the one hand it felt warm and cozy, and on the other it was as if Jade was still around making a posthumous statement.

Rider started reading a non-fiction book on his phone that he'd purchased a month earlier and never gotten around to, but he found it hard to concentrate and he wound up putting his phone away and staring into the fire for the next hour. As a writer he'd learned not to feel guilty about not reading for pleasure as much as other people. He spent the majority of his days writing or editing something, and when he wasn't working he thought it was counter-productive…and sometimes a little dangerous…to read someone else's writing. For the most part he preferred to read classic fiction so he could absorb the writing styles and the more technical aspects of the narrative.

When he realized it was almost midnight, he turned off the fireplace and headed for the stairs. His eyes had grown heavier and he started looking forward to sleeping for once. Dealing with everything since Jade had died had been more draining than he'd realized it would be. The only thing he wanted to do that night was climb into bed, pull up the covers and close his eyes until morning.

Ryan Field

He entered the bedroom slowly, without making a sound. There was enough light filtering through the windows so he could see Sandler turned on his side facing the window. Sandler appeared to be sleeping; he didn't move or turn when Rider entered. Now all Rider had to do was get undressed and slip into bed without being noticed. He didn't feel like having sex with Sandler that night, and he knew how enthusiastic Sandler could be about sex. Even though they hadn't had sex since Sandler met that frat guy at the town festival, Rider knew how aggressive guys like Sandler could be sometimes.

After he undressed, he climbed into bed with such ease the mattress barely moved at all. He made a point not to pull the covers up too fast. When he got his legs just right, he turned a little on his side facing in the opposite direction of Sandler so gently the covers hardly moved. On any other night he would have put the TV on for a few minutes, but he didn't want to risk the chance of waking Sandler...and his huge erection...and ruining his peace and quiet.

When he was finally settled, he closed his eyes and took a quick breath. He exhaled slowly. He didn't even turn and fluff his pillow, for fear he might arouse Sandler. The room was so silent he heard nothing but the sound of the furnace in a distant part of the building. His eyes

194

grew even heavier and he felt himself drifting off without even trying too hard, which was unusual for him.

Then the bed moved.

He felt a large warm hand rest on his naked bottom.

He rolled his eyes and said, "Not tonight, Sandler. I have a headache. Be a good boy and go to sleep."

The hand patted his bottom, and then squeezed it gently.

"I said not tonight, Sandler. I'm really not in the mood. If you're a good boy and go right back to sleep, I'll give you a blowie in the morning." He hated to treat him as if he were a child, but sometimes the most aggressive men behaved like children.

"Well that's not very encouraging," said a voice that wasn't Sandler's. "I had this feeling there would be all kinds of hot sex going on in this room tonight. *You* never say no to anyone."

Rider's eyes opened wide and he turned over fast. "What are *you* doing in here?" He was staring directly into Drew's large brown eyes.

"I asked Sandler to switch rooms with me tonight," Drew said. "He didn't mind in the least. But if I'd known you were going to be this grumpy I wouldn't have bothered. You sure do know how to ruin a moment."

Rider didn't know what to say. "I'm in shock. I didn't expect to find you in bed next to me. You never do things like that. You're the most predictable person I've ever known."

Drew smiled again. "Then we're even, because I never thought I'd see the day you turn down sex from anyone. Last I heard, you're ready and willing to please. I was feeling a little horny and I figured I'd come in here and *get some*. I guess I'll have to settle for one of your famous blow jobs in the morning."

When Drew said *that*, in that snarky, condescending tone, it felt as if Rider's entire body exploded into one huge mushroom of flames. He threw the covers down. He turned on a lamp on the night stand and jumped out of bed. As he crossed to the other side of the room, he said, "That's it. I have had enough. I'm tired of the slut-shaming and I'm tired of the innuendo."

Drew sat up in bed and just gaped at him without saying a word.

"That's right," Rider said. "I have had just about enough of it. I've admitted that I made more than a few mistakes when we were a couple. I've admitted that I wasn't faithful. I've even admitted that I do like my sex and I do like men, all kinds of men. That's right, I like it. I've apologized for what I did so many times I lost count. And I'm tired of apologizing for it. No. More. Apologies. I'm not the same person I was two years ago when we were a couple, and thankfully being here in Vermont has helped me realize that. If I had a little fun with Sandler while I've been here that's no one's business but mine and Sandler's. It's not as if I was cheating on you, because we haven't been a couple in a long time. And you have no right to shame me and no right to make me feel guilty about anything I've done, or might do in the future, as long as we're not a couple. *And for the record*, I'm tired of being treated as if I'm some kind of a sex maniac. I've said no to plenty of men in my life and I'm tired of you making me out to be some kind of bottom whore come dump that will lift up his legs for any man that asks."

"I'm sorry," Drew said. "I thought you knew I was only joking."

"Oh, you're not joking," Rider said. "You make it sound as if you're joking, but deep down you're really judging. And while we're on the topic, I'd like to get something else out in the open. One of the biggest issues we had while we were a couple is that I was never fully honest with you in bed and I don't think you were honest with me. We had good sex, but we never really explored everything we wanted and desired. There were times when I felt as if you were treating me like some kind of a delicate crystal object you were afraid to break."

Drew tilted his head sideways. "So you're mad at me for treating you with respect, dignity and kindness? You're mad that I didn't objectify you? For believing that you were more than just a piece of ass?"

"No," Rider said. "That's not what I'm saying." He walked back to the bed and lowered his voice. "All I'm saying is that we both treated each other as if we were terrified to do anything or say anything in bed that might scare the other away. We weren't as honest as we should have been and I think that hurt our relationship more than it helped it. I'll be totally honest right now, because I want to get this all out in the open. As much as I love the way you treated me, there are times when I want a man to just treat me like I'm a piece of ass. It's not reality, it's only fantasy. It's a little game that lovers play in bed. I like to be treated rough sometimes, and I like it when a man takes full control and I submit completely. If that makes me a bad person, I don't care anymore. I like my sex."

"Then why didn't you ever just say that?" Drew asked. "I'm not a mind reader."

Rider sat down on the edge of the bed and said, "Because I loved you too much. I was afraid to say it. I was afraid that if I said these things you'd think I was some kind of depraved sex slave lunatic."

This time Drew climbed out of bed and crossed to the other side of the room. "Well let me tell *you* something, Rider. You make me crazy sometimes. I'm not exactly the prude you think I am either. There were times when we were having sex that I wanted to bang you so hard you'd have bruises on the backs of your legs. I wanted to make you get down on your hands and knees and beg for it while I rubbed my feet all over your face. I have my kinks, too. That's right. I'm not just into sex in the missionary position. And do you know why I never let go that way, and why I never fucked you so hard you begged for mercy?"

"No. Why?"

Drew walked over to the bed and sat down next to him. He took a deep breath and exhaled. "Because I loved you so much I couldn't even imagine doing anything that might hurt you." He put his arm around him. "I've never loved anyone else like you. When I see you enter a room my heart stops and I have to concentrate on breathing again. God help me if I look into your blue eyes. Then it's all over."

Rider rested his head against Drew's chest and said, "Let me get this right. You're telling me that you really wanted to do dirty, sexy things to me. The things that I wanted you to do to me but was afraid to ask."

"Oh yes. I wanted to do the dirtiest things to you. And I felt so awful."

Rider smiled. "Well, maybe we should explore this now that we've gotten it all out in the open."

"What do you mean?"

"Okay, let's try this," Rider said. "What if I told you that I thought you have the biggest, hottest, sexiest feet on the planet, and that I'd like to get down on the floor and lick them?"

Drew laughed. "I'd wiggle my toes and tell you to get down on the fucking floor and lick."

"You'd actually use the F word?"

"Darn right I would."

"Darn?"

Drew laughed. "*Damn.*"

Without even realizing it, they'd both grown erect. Rider reached down between Drew's legs and wrapped his hand around his cock. He stroked him gently and said, "Did I ever tell you how much I like your hairy chest?"

"No."

He rubbed the bottom of Drew's dick with his thumb. "Did I ever tell you how much I love your hairy legs?"

"I was thinking of shaving them. Everyone's doing it."

"Don't you dare," Rider said. "I like a man with a little hair on his body and you've got just the right amount."

Drew turned and pushed him back onto the bed. As he climbed on top of him, he asked, "Did I ever tell you that I like your smooth legs?"

"No." He lifted his legs and spread them.

"Did I ever tell you how much I like your smooth round ass?"

Rider reached up to grab his shoulders. "No, never. But don't stop now." They'd never spoken this much during sex.

"I love everything about your hot little body," Drew said. "I always have and I always will. If I told you there's no other ass like it would you believe me?"

"No," Rider said. "I would think you're exaggerating because my ass is pretty normal. But go ahead and do it anyway. I like the way it sounds."

And that night, for the first time, they slipped into the kind of raw sex they'd always wanted but never had the courage to try. This time it was based on love, not fear. It wasn't always easy; old habits tend to stick around longer than they should sometimes. But it turned out to be more relaxed, and filled with more intimacy than Rider had ever known with Drew, or any other man. It wasn't totally based on what they said or did either. Even though they said a few dirty things, and exaggerated a little more than they'd done in the past, it was more about the unspoken connection they made that night that transcended the physical. For the first time, they weren't just acting out the expected, specific roles they'd always known, based only on the need to please the other. They grew together as one, pleasing themselves as much as they worked to please the other. And when it was over and Drew fell on top of Rider all sweaty and gasping for breath, Rider caressed the back of his head and told him again he didn't think it was possible to love anyone more than he loved him at that moment.

"I love you even more now than the first day I met you," Drew said.

"I want us to try again," Rider said. "I don't want to lose you all over again. And I need to know that. I can't wonder about it anymore."

"I don't want to lose you again either," Drew said.

"You never did."

CHAPTER FIFTEEN

"If you make me miss this flight you'll live to regret it," Drew said, as he paced back and forth near the front door of the craftsman cottage in West Hollywood.

"I'll be right out," Rider said. "We have plenty of time."

"Traffic will be heavy," Drew said. "We're going to miss this flight."

"You always say that," Rider said. Drew could be so compulsive at times.

"That's because you're always late for everything."

"I'm not late today," Rider said. "All I have to do is put on my underwear now."

"You're not even dressed yet?" Drew asked.

Rider laughed. "I'm just joking. I'm dressed. I'll be right out."

"Then what in the world are you doing in there?"

"I only have to put a few more things into my suitcase and I'm ready."

"You're not even packed yet?" Drew asked. "This is rich. I should have known and set the alarm an hour earlier. Or I should have just packed for you. From now on that's what I'll do. What on earth could you be doing so long in that bathroom?"

"I'm just tweaking my beard a little," Rider said. "Calm down." He was sorry he'd said that.

"Don't tell me to calm down."

"I'm sorry," he said. "But it's your fault. You're the one who wanted to have sex this morning. And now I have to take care of things so I don't look like a complete mess."

A moment later, Rider appeared in the living room with three suitcases and asked, "How do I look? I couldn't decide between the tan jacket or the black leather."

Drew walked over to where he was standing without looking at him and said, "You look fantastic." He grabbed two of the suitcases Rider was carrying. "Now let's go before we miss this flight. What on earth do you have in these heavy suitcases anyway? And why on earth did you pack so much?"

"I'll carry them myself if it's too much trouble," Rider said. "I need everything I packed. After all, I don't live here with you full time and it's not as if I have all my things at hand to pack. It's not easy going between my place and your place all the time."

Drew let that comment slip by and he stopped complaining, which Rider knew he would. After they'd returned from their trip to Vermont to do the feature with Jade and Thorn, they got back together as a couple. They'd defined their relationship as monogamous and things were working out better than even Rider had expected. It had been over nine months since they'd been to Vermont and they'd slipped back into their relationship as if it had never ended in the first place. It was almost too easy, which is why they both decided not to live together right away. They both thought it wiser to continue as a couple with separate living arrangements until they were both ready to make that commitment to live together. In the beginning it worked, and that was partly because they were both terrified to rush anything for fear they might spoil what they'd rekindled. However, that had been almost a year ago and Rider was getting tired of living out of suitcases in two different places.

Drew rarely came to his apartment, which made sense because it was only a studio and too small for two people to be comfortable. So Rider wound up spending the majority of his time staying at Drew's house. In the beginning he liked it because it was different and new, but now it was getting tired. There were mornings where he had to borrow things to wear from Drew, and he and Drew had completely different taste in clothes. There were mornings he went without underwear because he couldn't even find his. And there were some mornings when he woke up and didn't even remember whether he was in his apartment or Drew's house.

As they climbed into the backseat of the Uber car that was taking them to the airport, Rider settled into his seat and said, "If we lived together it would make things a lot easier." He didn't want to push the issue, but he did want to plant the thought in Drew's head. He'd been dropping hints for a while now.

The car pulled off and Drew said, "Or it might complicate things. You know how I feel about his. I thought we agreed to discuss it at a later date. Things are going well now and I don't want to ruin them."

Rider glanced toward the window and sighed. "That's fine. I'll never bring up the topic again. We can be roommates for the rest of our lives for all I care." Then he turned his entire body toward the window and looked at his phone.

After a few moments of silence, Drew said, "You're doing that thing again."

"What thing?" They were stuck in traffic and Rider was tweeting something to his followers.

"That thing you do that you know makes me feel guilty," Drew said. "You're ignoring me by staring at your phone and making those endless tweets."

"I have no idea what you're talking about," Rider said, as he looked down and sent his tweet. "I like to tweet. Some people do, some people don't. I do." He glanced down at his Twitter again. "People expect me to tweet. I have a fan base and it's good promotion for the web site."

"You're sulking and you're making me feel guilty about the fact that we're not living together," Drew said. "And stop looking at your Twitter."

Rider knew he couldn't rush him. He didn't want to rush him either. He knew this wasn't about Twitter either. As much as he wanted to move in together and start planning their wedding, he knew he had no choice but to wait until Drew was ready. Drew had always been more methodical and detail oriented. He had to plan and prepare and navigate his entire life the same way a tour guide navigates an Alaskan cruise. If Rider rushed Drew into anything he feared it might ruin everything they'd built so far.

He reached out and took Drew's hand in his and said, "I'm not sulking. I'm not trying to make you feel guilty about anything. I'm fine with our arrangement the way it is and I could probably do this for the rest of my life without complaining. It's just that it's not easy sometimes when practical matters come into play. It's not simple to go between two different places all the time, especially when you're planning for a trip."

"It's the beard," Drew said.

"*Huh?*"

"It's the beard that makes you later than usual all the time," Drew said. "You were always late for everything before, but ever since you've grown that beard you've been extra late."

"Are you saying that I'm high maintenance again?" Rider asked.

Drew laughed. "Well, you're not exactly low maintenance, with or without the beard."

Rider knew he had a point, so he ignored that comment and said, "I thought you liked my beard." A few months ago he'd decided to grow one of those trendy lumberjack beards. It had just reached the point where it was full and bushy like it should be. But it wasn't easy to maintain. He had to trim it just right and make sure nothing was uneven. For some odd reason, it always seemed easier to get the beard even on each individual side of his face, but close to impossible to keep both sides even.

"I like your face a lot better," Drew said. "I'm starting to miss your face. You know you don't have to follow every trend that comes along. You don't have to have a beard."

"Are you saying that I'm trendy?" Rider asked.

"Well there is that beard, and your pants are a little tight," Drew said. "I sometimes wonder how you can stand wearing those skinny jeans so tight. Sometimes I'm afraid I'll wake up next to a guy with a man bun."

Rider folded his arms across his chest and moved closer to the door. "Well."

Drew smiled and said, "Don't get mad. I must like it. After all, I put up with it."

"*You put up with it?*"

"I don't mean it like that," Drew said. "I'm just saying that I think everything you do is special in one way or another, even if it's trendy or annoying."

"*Annoying?*"

"You know I don't mean it in a bad way," Drew said. "Look the traffic is starting to move. You'd better tweet something before we get to the airport."

Rider glanced down at his phone again, without replying. He knew Drew wasn't being mean on purpose and he'd learned how to parse most of the things he said by then. Drew had the uncanny ability to say the most innocent things at the most inappropriate times and wind up insulting people. It's not that he planned it. It was never done in a mean-spirited way. He just couldn't help the fact that his foot often wound up stuck in his proverbial mouth.

Of course they arrived at the airport an hour earlier than they should have, thanks to Drew's obsessive compulsive desire to never be late for anything. Rider didn't say anything. He just sat and waited until it was time to board. This trip back to Vermont was too important to cloud with silly issues like being too early or tweeting in traffic. The main reason they were heading to Vermont was for a memorial service that

Thorn had planned for Jade. It wasn't a large memorial either. As far as Rider knew, it would only be the two of them, plus Thorn, Aunt Betty, and Sandler.

Rider hadn't seen Sandler in almost six months. As Rider had predicted at the time, Sandler's relationship with the frat guy, Bret, never amounted to much. However, after Sandler did the porn film with Thorn's studio, he quit working for the web site and moved to Vermont full time to work in adult entertainment. Although it was a shocking move for most of the people who knew Sandler, it didn't totally shock Rider. He knew better than any of them how much Sandler loved his sex, especially when he was the aggressive top.

The memorial service in Vermont wasn't the only reason they were leaving LA that morning. After the service, Thorn would drive them down to New York where they would meet Boris at one of the most prestigious LGBTQ awards ceremonies in the world. When their web site launched, and people read the feature Rider had written about Jade and Thorn, they went viral the first week and ever since then they were one of the most popular online sources for LGBTQ content. Without even trying too hard, they rivaled the biggest names in online journalism, both LGBTQ and mainstream. And that year Rider's story about Jade and Thorn had been nominated for an award in digital journalism and Boris wanted everyone there in person in case they won. Rider had become one of the most popular online openly gay journalists, and his regular column had millions of followers.

When they finally arrived in Vermont, Thorn drove down to the airport personally to pick them up. They spotted his large black Bentley immediately, and he jumped out of the car and started waving at them. He looked pretty much the same, except for the fact that he'd grown a bushy, trendy beard, too. The only difference between his beard and Rider's were more gray hairs, and he'd stopped dying his hair jet black.

On the way back to the renovated barn, Drew and Thorn talked nonstop until they pulled into the driveway. Rider sat in the backseat and listened without saying much. He noticed a small change in Thorn. Now that Jade was gone Thorn didn't seem as confident and he didn't tell as many long, endless stories. For the most part, though, Rider was more interested in the way Drew was answering Thorn's questions about them as a couple than he was in adding anything to the conversation. As usual, Drew replied to all of Thorn's questions with well-thought out replies that were so ambiguous they could have been mistaken for fiction. He also kept looking back at Rider, with a wink and a smile, each time Thorn asked about when they were going to get married.

Rider said nothing. He just returned the smiles and listened closely because he knew if he pushed Drew too hard into marriage...or even living together...he might lose him altogether. And the truth was he was okay with that, at least for the time being. It's just that each time Drew answered one of Thorn's questions with a blank reply about marriage he didn't have to appear so damn carefree and happy about it.

At dinner that night, they caught up with Sandler and Aunt Betty. Sandler seemed thrilled with what he was doing in the adult entertainment industry, both the acting and the production work. Thorn even praised his tech skills and said Sandler had helped them save thousands of dollars on tech support. Rider just listened and smiled. He'd seen a few of the adult films that Sandler had done over the past year and he couldn't get some of the images out of his head no matter how hard he tried. Whenever he thought about the fact that he'd taken Sandler's huge penis the way those guys in the movies were taking him now, his heart started to race a little faster.

The morning following their arrival they all gathered in the front hall for Jade's memorial service. No one dressed formally because Thorn had made it clear it was supposed to be informal. Thorn even said that if the circumstances had been different and he'd never met Drew and Rider, he would most likely have done his own very small memorial service alone. That's the way Jade had wanted it. And the only reason Drew and Rider were there was because Thorn felt so close to them. The only one who wore black was Aunt Betty, which she claimed was a show of respect. Even then, after all those months had passed, she still appeared visibly shaken over Jade's death in a way that was so unlike her. She didn't speak much, and never complained once.

As promised, the ceremony was simple and didn't last longer than fifteen minutes. Thorn read a favorite piece from Jade's collection of Kahlil Gibran, and then ended with another short Gibran quote. After that, he scattered Jade's ashes into the stream and everyone turned and headed back to the barn.

Rider felt at peace. He thought it was the perfect tribute to Jade: plain and simple, without a hint of pretense, just the way Jade would have wanted it.

The only one who seemed a little confused was Aunt Betty. On the way back to the barn she asked, "So that's it? No music. No cake. Nothing?"

Thorn reached for her elbow to help her along and said, "That's it. I'm afraid that's the way Jade wanted things and I'm only following his instructions."

She thought for a moment, and then said, "I see. Just don't do anything like that for me when it's my time, dear. I want the works, limousines and all."

They left for New York in Thorn's Bentley right after the memorial. It was a long drive from Northern Vermont to Manhattan and they didn't want to miss the awards ceremony. Aunt Betty remained in Vermont, and so did Sandler. Aunt Betty had no interest in long road trips, and Sandler remained behind because they were in the middle of filming a new adult film that he was directing.

There was an accident on the New York Thru-way and they wound up sitting in traffic for almost two hours. When they finally arrived in Manhattan, they pulled up to the front of the building where Boris lived and Boris's doorman parked the car for them in a garage. They had less than an hour to get dressed for the ceremony and to get there on time.

This was only a one night deal in New York, so they were staying at Boris's apartment that night instead of a hotel. The next morning

215

Thorn was driving back to Vermont and Rider and Drew had a flight back to LA. While Boris showed Thorn to his bedroom, Rider and Drew went to their room on their own because they'd stayed there many times in the past.

"Just put on your formal suit and don't waste any time," Drew said, as he dropped his pants and removed his shirt.

"Well I have to use the bathroom," Rider said. "I know you don't care about how your hair looks, but I care about how mine looks and I need at least five minutes to fix things. I'm a complete mess. I've been sitting in a car all day."

Drew sighed. "You get five minutes, and you're leaving the door open so I can see what you're doing. We don't have much time and I don't want to show up late. After all, this is your big night."

"Well then if it's my big night why are you making me nervous," Rider said. "You know that when you make me nervous it only takes longer to get ready. It's very defeatist, Drew."

Drew walked over to him and kissed his cheek. "Look, sweetheart. Let's not waste time bickering. Just go into the bathroom and do whatever it is you do in there."

Rider nodded and said, "Okay. I'll only be a minute."

As he crossed into the bathroom, Drew called out his name and said, "You actually look wonderful right now. You've never looked better. You could go just like this if you wanted to."

Rider glanced back. "I do?"

"Yes," Drew said. "In fact, for some reason, you haven't looked this great in ages."

Rider smiled and said, "Nice try." He knew Drew was only saying that to get him to move along faster.

"It's the truth," Drew said. "You're always the best looking guy in the room to me."

"But I'm not good enough to marry, or to live with," Rider said. He figured that was a good time to slip that comment into the conversation.

"You said that, not me. And in case you didn't notice, we already are practically living together."

"It's not the same and you know it," Rider said. "I want a home and a family of my own. I might even want to cook things." Then he turned and headed into the bathroom without waiting for Drew to reply. He didn't want to get into that discussion at that moment. He only wanted to mention it again so Drew would know how he felt.

A few hours later, as Rider sat there waiting to see if he'd won the award for his category, he found it amusing that so much had changed in the past year. Most of all, he'd changed and a lot of that had to do with meeting Jade and Thorn. They'd helped him see that two extremely different gay men can have a lifelong relationship, both emotionally and now legally. He'd worked out many of the issues he'd had with Drew and their sex life by just learning to be honest and express his true feelings. They were still at that stage where they couldn't get enough of each other, however, Thorn had mentioned that it doesn't last forever and every relationship that moves forward starts to rely less on sex and more about the intimacy. And that was okay, too. Rider didn't mind. He found it even more amusing that he was looking forward to growing old with Drew, even though Drew didn't seem quite as excited as he did.

Rider didn't win the award that night, which left everyone else around him frowning far more than he did. He didn't care about awards. Just being nominated for the award had been nice enough, but it's not something he needed to remain focused professionally. If anything, he silently sighed in relief when he didn't win. He still had so much more to do that it would have felt awkward to win something this soon in his career. The gay woman who won had written a wonderful piece on feminism and discrimination in the workplace, and frankly he thought she deserved to win more than he did.

As the ceremony started to wind down, Rider leaned over to Drew and said, "Maybe we should all leave now while the going is good. This way we don't have to talk to anyone on the way out."

Drew looked at him and shook his head. "We can't leave now. The ceremony isn't over yet and it wouldn't look good. Besides, I want to see what's next. I heard there's some kind of surprise at the end."

"Oh right," Rider said. He'd never been more bored in his life. "What's the surprise? Is Dan Savage going to yodel a Bette Midler Christmas song with Rainbow Randy?"

"It's Randy Rainbow, not Rainbow Randy."

"I don't give a shit. I'm bored."

Drew laughed and said, "Just be quiet and sit still."

Fifteen or twenty minutes later, at the exact moment Rider was ready to get up and leave, Boris stood up and climbed up on the main stage. As he adjusted the microphone, and the audience grew silent, Rider quelled the urge to yawn and focused on the stage. He had no idea that Boris would say anything that night.

After he introduced himself to the audience, and explained that he owned Rainbow Palm Productions, which owned *The Rainbow Times*, the audience applauded. When the applause died down, Boris cleared his throat and said, "And now for a special surprise ending to a wonderful evening." Then he gestured toward Drew and Rider's table.

Even though he had no idea what was happening, Rider smiled and sent Drew a look.

Drew stood up from the table and reached into his pocket.

Someone from backstage came down with a microphone and stood beside Drew.

"What's going on?" Rider asked.

Drew stepped up to where Rider was seated and got down on one knee. As he reached forward with a small box in his right hand, the guy put the microphone up to his mouth. Then Drew cleared his throat, looked into Rider's eyes, and said, "Will you marry me?"

People started talking photos.

Boris applauded on stage and everyone joined him.

Drew remained on one knee, looking into Rider's eyes, waiting for him to reply.

Rider had never been rendered speechless in his life. He'd never expected this to happen and he felt completely overwhelmed. He reached out and took the small box from Drew. When he opened it he saw two identical gold wedding bands studded with small diamonds.

Drew asked again, "Will you marry me?"

Rider felt a tear slide down his cheek. He leaned forward and reached for Drew's hand. "Of course I'll marry you." Then he fell into his arms and kissed him so hard the guy standing next to Drew dropped the microphone.

The audience continued to applaud, but they sounded faint and distant to Rider. "I can't believe you did this. How long was this planned?"

Drew helped him stand up and said, "Weeks. I was terrified you'd find out."

"I can't believe I didn't find out."

"I was also terrified you might say no."

Rider smiled. He grabbed the small ring box from Drew and said, "Give me my ring." As he slipped it onto his finger, he put his arm around Drew and said, "I'm never taking this off again. I'll die with this ring on my finger." He meant that, and he knew he wouldn't remove it again.

After that, Boris joined them at the table and he and Drew started talking about the wedding plans that Drew had made. Evidently, they weren't going to have a long engagement. Drew had planned for them all to drive back up to Vermont the next morning so they could get married in Thorn and Jade's barn.

At first, Drew seemed a little worried that Rider might be upset he'd made all these plans without consulting him first. Rider only smiled and wiped a tear from his face. The fact that Drew had gone through all that trouble was enough in itself. If he'd planned a wedding at a fast food restaurant Rider wouldn't have minded. The only thing he cared about was marrying the man he'd been in love with for the past five years, and spending the rest of his days with the man he would always love more than life itself.

ABOUT THE AUTHOR

Ryan Field is a gay fiction writer who has worked in many areas of publishing for the past 20 years. He's the author of the bestselling "Virgin Billionaire" series and the short story, "Down the Basement," which was included in the Lambda Award winning anthology titled "Best Gay Erotica 2009." Though not always, he sometimes writes gay parodies of *straight* mainstream fiction/films in the same way straight fiction and Hollywood has been parodying gay men for years, without apology. He also writes hetero romances with pen names, and has edited several short story anthologies. "Chase of a Lifetime," is his first self-published 99-cent Amazon Kindle book. It's a 60,000 word full length novel in the gay erotic romance genre.

He has a long list of publishing credits that include over 100 works of lgbt fiction, some with pen names in various sub-genres. His e-mail is listed, and he welcomes all comments, or through e-mail. Please check out his web site for updates. www.ryan-field.blogspot.com You can reach at mailto:rfieldj@aol.com Follow Facebook Fan Page: Books by Ryan Field https://www.facebook.com/Books-by-Ryan-Field-112186572328/

OTHER TITLES BY RYAN FIELD

A Life Filled with Awesome Love
A Regular Bud
A Sign from Heaven Above
A Young Widows Promise
All About Yves
American Star
American Star II
An Officer and His Gentleman
Another Regular Bud
Baby Cakes
Big Bad And On Top
Billabong Bang
Bury it Officer
Cage James
Capping the Season
Captain Velvet's Velvet Box
Cherry Soda Cowboy
Cowboy Christmas Miracle
Cowboy Howdy
Cowboy Mike and Buddy Boy
Dancing Dirty
Dirty Little Virgin
Field of Dreams
Four Feet Under
Four Gay Weddings and a Funeral
Gay Pride and Prejudice
He's Bewitched
Hot Italian Lover
Internal Desires
It's Nice to be Naughty

OTHER TITLES BY RYAN FIELD

OTHER TITLES BY RYAN FIELD

Unabated

Uncertainty

Unmentionable: The Men Who Loved on the Titanic

Vance's Flame

Whatever Dude

When A Man Loves A Man

When Harry Met Sal

With this Cowboy I Love so Freely

You Missed a Spot Big Guy

Young Doughy Joey

Young Hung and Hitched

Bad Boy Billionaire Series:

Cowboy in Love

Palm Beach Sex Scandal

Silicon Valley Sex Scandal

Small Town Romance Writer

The Actor Learning to Love

The Ivy League Rake

The Vegas Shark

The Wall Street Shark

Chase Series:
Chase of a Christmas Dream

Chase of a Dream - Abridged

Chase of a Dream - Unabridged

Chase of a Holy Ghost

Chase of a Lifetime

Chase of an Adventure: Fifty Shades of Gay

Down The Basement Series:

Down the Basement

Down the Basement II: Santa Saturday

OTHER TITLES BY RYAN FIELD

Second Chance Series:
Second Chance
Second Chance: His Only Choice
Second Chance: The Littlest Christmas Tree
Second Chance: The Sweetest Apple

The Virgin Billionaire Series:
The Virgin Billionaire
The Virgin Billionaire and the Evil Twin
The Virgin Billionaire: Revenge
The Virgin Billionaire's Dream House
The Virgin Billionaire's Hot Amish Escapade
The Virgin Billionaire's Little Angel
The Virgin Billionaire's Reversal of Fortune
The Virgin Billionaire's Secret Baby
The Virgin Billionaire's Sexcellent Adventure
The Virgin Billionaire's Wedding

Riverdale Press Titles:
A Christmas Carl
Valley of the Dudes

Made in the USA
Las Vegas, NV
08 November 2021